No Trouble at All

Cursed Morsels Press

Contents

Notice of Content Warnings

Content warnings for each story are available in the back of the book.

Foreword

R.J. Joseph

We have all likely heard the admonishment that we can "catch more flies with honey than with vinegar," or some variation. Ideals of a polite citizenry ring throughout schools for small children, dinner conversations with teenagers, and pillow talk between partners. Syrupy sweetness, often the foundation for being polite, can be uplifting, sometimes—when it is genuine.

When it is not authentic, politeness sours, decaying our souls just as surely as sugar decays tooth enamel. Insincerity weakens our defenses the way high levels of sugar in the blood inhibit white blood cells. Niceties can cut more deeply than outright slashes with a knife because of their subversive nature. We never see it coming.

Demands for respectability and civility are often weaponized against marginalized communities, used to sow division and perpetuate inequitable institutions such as misogyny, patriarchy, capitalism, racism, ableism, homophobia—we can select from any of these abuses and find ways respectability politics uphold the practices. The insistence on victims speaking in an amiable tone to those who wish to keep them subjugated places the onus on the oppressed to beg their freedom from the oppressors.

The requirement for those who are trespassed against to address injustices through civil discourse promulgates the false idea that everyone is engaging in these discourses in good faith. "If only they were nicer, and did not so speak harshly, maybe they would not be in the situations they are in." These mandates for politeness are not always made in good faith.

More often, the true goal is to use civility as a mask for ill treatment, exploitation, and cruelty.

The authors in this anthology understand the way good manners, or at least, the appearance of such, provides the perfect weapon for victims and marginalized communities to use in search of their freedom: in asserting their independence and desire to break away from the binds that hold them unjustly. Just as civility can work as a mask to cover grief a community does not know how to—or even desire to—address, it can also become a mask to veil true intentions towards seeking selfhood.

As a result, women being forced to sacrifice themselves and their rights, in upholding the status quo, all for the sake of being regarded as "nice girls", or small children feeling afraid of their family's alienation if they don't behave "nicely" conveniently backfires with bad faith actors who care nothing for their victims' politeness. Embittered communities, treated poorly by their non-agreed upon leaders, must mask their pain with sweet words and deference they do not feel—nor should be required to give. These tales achingly reveal what politeness can hide. And they subvert the expectations that being polite can solve any problems.

When faced with the choice between saving themselves or succumbing to the inauthenticity of forced courteousness, some of the characters in these stories choose themselves. Their freedom in a world that no longer exists, or that changes drastically, means more to them than bondage in one where they will never be free.

These fifteen expertly woven, nuanced tales are presented with all the cloying saccharine sweetness found in the most courteous interactions. However, make no mistake. These are the kind of honey that catches dastardly flies and leads them to their tortured demise.

May 2023

Cire Perdue

Ariel Marken Jack

It's February when I realize my legs are made of wax. It's not the month that comes as a surprise to me—nothing good ever happens in February—but it's a shock somehow to discover the season has changed. The last I noticed, it was November, the season of things dying brittle and gone to grey. Now the world is salt slush and nothing has ever lived. Only the grey and the gone remain the same.

I am melting into the floor in front of the battered washer that reigns over our basement like the figurehead of a ship. A moth sizzles black on the bare bulb hanging overhead. My flatmate is on the stairs, talking. I am pretending to take what she says to heart.

"You should report him," Andromeda says. "Really, Valerie. He shouldn't get away with it."

I nod, but we both know I won't. My faded red overalls peel off my unwashed body like the skin of a spoiled fruit. I stuff them into the washer's discoloured porthole, shove the stiff hatch shut, imagine wintering aboard a seafaring vessel—swaying across oceans of salt water instead of slogging through grit-scattered streets.

My soft knees are stained from the potting soil that was ground through the work-worn denim. Their caps are dented and deformed. I shed my sweater, then everything else I am wearing.

His smell lingers on my skin. Sour musk, printer toner, sweet floral soap—that last, his wife's choice, I imagine. He isn't the type to pay attention to the details that make life pretty. He has us to do that for him. Her and me and anyone else who lets him take whatever keeps him afloat throughout this season of saline corrosion. I push my thumbs into my knees, deepening the dents. The washer sputters on with a tidal slosh.

The shower's intense heat softens my paraffin bones. I slide down the tiled soap scum wall and crumple into the tub. The beer Andromeda fetched from the freezer as I walked naked from the basement through the kitchen feels like an icicle in my grasp, but the cold solidifies my too-yielding fingers. I drink it half down in a single dizzying pull. It's only Wednesday. Three more shifts until my week is over. My phone dings, muffled in the bathmat. I swipe a soapy finger to see what Kevin has to say. I know it's Kevin before I read the text. No one else texts when I get home from work to check if I managed to evade the manager again.

He caught me as I was clocking out. I wish Kevin worked as late as I do, but we can't persuade the owners to align our schedules. They claim there aren't enough customers late in the day to justify keeping two employees on the floor. That hasn't been my experience, but there's no arguing with people who know how much they own.

The text says, *Valerie! You get out ok?* I drop the phone back to the mat so I don't have to tell him *not this time*. Andromeda always knows these things without me having to say. It's one of the reasons I don't think I could live with anyone else. Not after her.

I'd managed to avoid letting him catch my eye for weeks. I hadn't looked him in the face since the last time. I'm not perfect, though. I got careless. I forgot to be on the store phone, tidying a display, buried in my work—any work—when he came out of his office. He smiled when he saw me looking at him. He asked if I had a minute. He said my name wrong. No one else ever calls me Val.

I followed him into the back room and dutifully listened. I'm a good listener. He told me all of his problems, again. They weren't my problems, or problems with me. I've been employee of the month six months in a row.

The bath is shimmering with soap and melted skin. The water builds up in our tub because we still haven't fixed the drain. The stopper falls down on its own. You have to hold it up with a bottle cap if you don't want to stew. Andromeda opened my beer for me. The cap must be in the kitchen. The bottle is empty. I don't re-member swallowing. My legs waver under the surface, bending like light refracted through lightning-struck sand. Underwater, they look more oceanic—like coral, or kelp—than human. I wonder how they will look if I ever emerge.

I could have said no. I could have gone home. His problems weren't special. I'd heard them before—the dull job, the crying baby, the wife with no time for him. The necessity of something just for himself. Oh, *you* understand, Val. You're such a good pal. Such a great gal. Maybe that's why. I'm nothing special, either. Maybe people who aren't special are supposed to stick together.

Andromeda doesn't understand things like that. She's never been anything but special. Andromeda could never be unspecial enough to let her manager at the garden centre, where she would never be unspecial enough to work at in the first place, take most of her clothes off, one article at a time, until the straps of her overalls dangled down her thighs and the potting soil heaps on the cool cement floor were obscured by clumps of thrift-store merino and the type of little crocheted accessories he said drove men so far out of their minds they couldn't be blamed for their actions. She wouldn't be so invested in keeping people happy—employee of the month, after all—that she wouldn't have known what else to do but let it happen. She wouldn't understand that it wasn't really all that bad.

I shake spruce-scented salts into the bath and think about the road salt spatter-ing the glossy steel of my nearly-new bicycle's frame. Its paint is midnight blue. The hot girl at the bike shop promised that if I took care of my new ride, it would last the rest of my life. I've been riding it all winter and still haven't oiled the chain. It squeaked like a mouse in a glue trap all the way home. The blue has vanished under layers of street-streaked grey.

As I slunk out the *employees only* door, something shifted inside my left knee. A shock of unseasonable heat swelling weakness into my pumping calves. I coasted most of the way home, but the feeling grew even after I eased up on the pedals. I didn't know what it meant until I saw what my knees looked like under the soil-stained overalls. "I'll wash you tomorrow," I promise. The bike is in the hall and there's no way it can hear me, but I have to fix *something*.

"I think that creep from the art college is stalking me again," Andromeda says when I finally make it out of the bath. My legs refuse to straighten. Thank goodness it's Andromeda's turn to cook. All I have to do is put on music. My flatmate likes to dance while she dishes. I collapse into my chair, plug my phone into the speakers some trust-fund painter traded for a loaf of Andromeda's homemade bread, stab my finger into the pixels of a random playlist.

A thin furrow delves between her perfect brows. "Will you come meet me after class? I'm modelling at seven."

I went to one of the drop-in drawing sessions she models for at the community centre in between classes at the college once, after she suggested I might need an artistic outlet. She stopped suggesting it after she saw what I drew.

"I would," I say, "But—" I pull up the edge of the towel and gesture at my knees.

One of Andromeda's other strays once said her knees looked like the knees of a victorious angel in a Renaissance painting. I don't know what that means, but everything about her looks like a painting to me. I've never been completely sure she's real. She's never worked a real job, anyway. In summer, when the art classes aren't in session, she makes her living off tourists. She paints herself bronze and stands on a pedestal down by the scenic end of the waterfront, changing poses in imperceptibly slow motion. She's never cooked what I would call real food. On my nights we eat lasagne and lentil soup. On her nights we eat nettles, glass noodles, raindrop cakes in which she's suspended flowers and berries she found in some forest she asked some painter to drive her to when they should have been painting her again.

She looks at my malformed kneecaps. "Oh. I'll ask Luka. You don't need to worry about me. I'll make you a salve for those when we get home. Here, try this and tell me how it is." She sets a red bowl of black rice with black beans, black sesame, black garlic, and papaya seeds added for spicy black crunch in front of me. I guess tonight is goth night. Must be Luka is the goth one. There's always a goth one. Andromeda likes a dark backdrop to bring out her shine.

Painters and sculptors and singers flow through our flat like a river of tithes and fantastical tributes. They bring her strange herbal spirits, metallic pigments, vintage silk robes. I don't know if they're more invested in persuading her to sleep with them or pose for the work that they hope will make them famous. I guess it doesn't have to be one or the other. I wonder if she knows I've tried to hate her and failed.

The flat is too quiet once Andromeda leaves. I sit in my towel and shiver against the table. My empty bowl is stained with black crumbs I should wash before they harden and have to be soaked. My knees are still too warm. I push a finger into the left one. It leaves a smooth-edged hole. I hope Andromeda's salve gets me back on my feet. I can't afford to take a day off.

———◇———

"No worries," Kevin says when I ask him to arrange the new potting mix display. "It's fine, Valerie, stop apologizing."

I can't tell him the real reason I'm not able to lift the heavy bags. Reliable coworkers don't say things like *my legs turned into wax, and now they're not great at bearing weight.* I adjust the drugstore braces that imply there is something normal wrong with my knees. I rode the bus to work, even though I worried I would melt all over the seat and blister the stranger sitting beside me, who probably didn't deserve to be burned. I still haven't washed my bike. Six hours until I get off. I see the manager lurking in his office, but he doesn't come out. I give Kevin half of my sandwich. He gives me a wink.

Andromeda is waiting when I lurch out the employee entrance. "Thought you might need a shoulder to lean on," she says. "This is Luka. He's strong! Use him as you like."

I look up. There's plenty of Luka. He's definitely the current goth one, but he hits the gym more than the previous goth one. I pretend not to see that his smile reveals a point of implanted fang. He feels steady like a boulder as he helps me across the icy lot and into the matte black leather interior of his flat black car.

"It's actually quite common," Dorothea says at dinner. She rests her plate on the mossy arm of our emerald velvet couch so she can talk with her hands. I see now why Luka has been assigned to me. He's being displaced. They can never bear to leave Andromeda's orbit, so she gives them little jobs. That way they can feel like they still matter. He settles his big arm around my shoulders and stares at Dorothea. I wonder if the heat I feel is coming from him or from the burning thing inside me.

Andromeda rustles across the room in layers of silk and dry leaves, her nacreous hands curled around the crossed stems of a quartet of slender wine glasses. "What's common, Dora?"

"Women turning to wax. I've heard about it before. It's got something to do with eternal girlhood. Internalized sense of the necessity of idealized malleability. Caving to social pressures. That sort of thing. They call it *Cire Perdue* Syndrome. Apparently it's quite a normal response in women who don't know how to—"

Andromeda presses a glass into one of Dorothea's floating hands. She takes the other hand and places it on her own waist, distracting Dorothea into silence before she says what I might be so commonly reacting to. What I don't know. What kind of woman I am. Luka's arm tightens. Something in my blazing shoulder gives.

On Thursday, Kevin is always between me and the office. I make myself meet his eyes and laugh at his jokes. I make myself smile at him after the manager cruises past my register, sees Kevin nearby, and returns to the office. He gives me a look that says *I know something's up, but don't take it out on me.* He's right. It isn't his fault. I give him my whole sandwich. I can't eat it myself—my fingers bent sideways when I tried to pry open the container.

Luka takes me home again. "Don't worry about it," he says, when I try to thank him. "I was driving past anyway." The stereo in his car is playing glitchy electronic echoes that sound like something Andromeda would have cooked to before she met Dorothea and switched to classical piano. I wonder if she remembers our bluegrass phase, back when we first moved to the city and wanted to play up our rural charms for the North End hipsters. When we slept in the same bed and held hands everywhere we went. I wonder if she remembers that my red overalls used to be hers, before she met Robin and traded overalls and bluegrass and me for Child Ballads and velvet gowns. I wonder if she remembers how things were with any of us. I wonder if she remembers Robin at all. She's so good at moving on.

Kevin texts me a sandwich emoji and a cat face with hearts for eyes. It was a good sandwich. I tell myself that's all he means. I reply with the plainest smiley. I don't know how to discourage him without being mean.

Friday evening, Andromeda says we're going out to celebrate surviving the week.

"We did good," she says. "No one murdered us! Let's live a little." She bends me into one of her vintage dresses. It wouldn't have fit a week ago—the boned and beaded midsection is stiff, unforgiving—but now my body gives. She gently moulds my waist to curve with the seams. "Gorgeous," she says, turning me to the mirror. "Look!"

Dorothea, standing in the doorway of my flatmate's tapestried bedroom, looks at Andromeda. "Yes," she agrees. "Gorgeous." Andromeda whirls me out of the bedroom, and Dorothea follows.

It starts to snow while we stand on the stoop, waiting for Luka to pick us up. The fleeting whiteness adorns Andromeda's hair with intricate constellations. It melts where it touches my skin. I think I hear it hiss into steam. Dorothea brushes Andromeda's starflakes away. I tilt my head back and open my mouth. I want the chilly sky to crawl inside me.

Luka half-carries me down the steps to the car. He opens my door, tucks me into the passenger seat. "Shotgun's for someone who likes me," he says, when Dorothea protests. She slinks into the back. I don't know why she even wants shotgun. Andromeda always sits in the back. I wonder if I do like him, or if I just understand him. They're not quite the same thing.

The waitress sets us in a distressed leather booth. It's a very Andromeda place. The decor is half landfill, half forest, familiar objects made alien by unsettling juxtapositions. Luka and Dorothea face each other at the outer ends of the horseshoe. Neither one smiles. The candles in the middle of the table burn high. The heat from Luka's body makes it impossible to ignore the magma inside mine. My hands go soft at the ends of my drooping arms. I drop a forkful of kale salad down the neckline of Andromeda's castoff dress. The heat from the candles follows the leaf down into the tight recesses between steel-boned brocade and deliquescing flesh. I am burning all over now. My legs grow so hot that my stockings begin to melt and run down my calves. I will not survive if I do not touch cold water.

"Excuse me." No one is looking. Luka slides out and allows me past, but his eyes never leave the spot on the table where Dorothea's hand is clawed across Andromeda's. I wobble to the ladies' room. I do not dare look down to see if I am dripping onto the floor. It feels as though every eye in the restaurant—even the flat dead eye of the plated fish waltzing by in a waiter's arms—has come to rest on the ruins of my borrowed finery. I don't actually think anyone is looking at all. I lean against the sink, running the cold tap over my wrists. My cell phone dings.

⚫

On Monday, the manager leans on my counter while Kevin gets ready to leave. Kevin comes out of the washroom and says that he must have dropped his wallet somewhere in the store. We spend the rest of my shift looking.

"Thanks," I say, when we finally flip the sign and lock the back door from outside.

"No problem," he says. "You'd do the same for me."

I wonder if I would. He gives me a quick hug before his bus rolls up. I can't be rude. I hug him back.

On Wednesday—Kevin's day off—I sit on a bale of peat during lunch and feel the manager staring at my naked feet. I kicked my clogs off to cool my toes in a perlite spill while I drink the smoothie Andromeda packed for my lunch. "Val, you can stay late tonight? I could really use some help." He explains about an order I know was placed last week. I wonder if he can tell that, under my sweater, my torso has slid a few degrees to the right. I wonder if he would ever look again if he saw my nakedness now, the lumps and drips, the indentations from everything I touch. The vein of ice from the smoothie sits crookedly inside me. I wonder how long Andromeda will keep reshaping me. I text her an S.O.S. but first I have to chill my fingertips against the frosted window, so they don't just squish across my phone's cracked screen.

"So sorry," I tell the manager when I leave. "I feel awful about the order, it's just my flatmate, she's having—well, it's personal. Lady stuff." The manager looks up at Luka and doesn't protest.

On Thursday, Kevin asks if I want to get Friday drinks. "I'll hang around until after your shift," he says. "We'll get out of here together. Blow off some steam." I don't want to get Friday drinks. I don't want to see Kevin outside work, but I know I owe him.

"Oh, I say. "I don't really drink, but maybe just one?"

He winks. "Don't worry. I'm not a creep."

I don't know why Dorothea has to be at the other end of the bar. I try to drown in my flight, grateful for the chilliness of these tiny glasses of weird experimental beers. I used to come here with Andromeda. Kevin talks about work. I nod as he recalls all the times he came between me and the manager. I wonder how quickly I can leave without being a bitch.

"I'll be sure to tell Luka I ran into you," Dorothea says when I pass by her on my way out. "Just, ah, chilling? With your ..."

"Coworker," I say. "From the garden centre."

She gives me a knowing look. She doesn't know me. "Do you know why they call it *Cire Perdue*?" she says, "Lost wax—if you don't know any French." She does a thing with her eyebrow, which I interpret as certainty that I would not know any French. "Look it up. Maybe warn your date not to get too attached."

I don't understand what Andromeda sees in her. I don't usually hate the painters this much. They're usually nicer to me, though. I think the observant ones see me as a second-best-case scenario and they want to figure out my secrets. She kept me around. She doesn't always do that.

———————⊙———————

"Dorothea says she saw you on a date," Andromeda says. She flips an amaranth waffle onto my plate. We always have waffles for Sunday brunch when it's just the two of us without any hangers-on. She tops it with a fan of mandarin slices, a drizzle of pomegranate molasses. "You didn't tell me you were seeing anyone! Did you have a good time?"

My hands feel too weird to steer the fork and knife. I break off pieces with my fingers. Andromeda eats with her hands to keep me company. She makes it look correct. The mandarin rind bites my tongue with oily spray.

"It was just drinks with Kevin from work. He asked. I couldn't say no." She gives me a knowing look. It's fine. She isn't Dorothea. She really knows me.

"You can always say no." Maybe she can. She doesn't remember how ordinary people have to live.

My phone chimes. I ignore it until it chimes again and I turn to pick it up.

"No, let me." She swipes it out of reach and squiggles my pattern across the screen. I would change the lock, but it's easier to let her know. She scowls. "The nerve. Look, this is what happens when you let them make assumptions." She slides it back across the table.

Dinner tonight. My place. I'll make eggplant parm. My grandma's recipe. You'll like it.

I don't like eggplant parmesan. I don't want to see anyone from work when I'm not getting paid. Maybe it would have been okay if he hadn't followed *You'll like it* with an eggplant emoji and a winking smiley face. I wonder if it was the

sandwiches. If I gave him ideas. My grandmother used to say that the fastest way
to a man's zipper was through his stomach. I used to cringe at that. I guess I should
have listened. My phone keeps chiming all day. I lie on the floor while Andromeda
does yoga, and let the battery die.

By dinnertime I am too soft to leave the flat. We eat at home. Dorothea fixes the
salad. One of my teeth smears against an iron-sided pumpkin seed. I push the rest
of my salad toward Luka. I'm grateful to Andromeda for decorating the flat with
mirrors. I turn to the nearest one to fix my tooth.

We're swigging Vinho Verde from the bottle. My wax is smeared across Luka's
lower lip. Andromeda declared everyone had to drink cold things in solidarity
with me. Dorothea is sulking. She wanted mulled wine. I can see her point—it's
February, after all—but the disappointment doesn't seem to stop her from drinking her share. The blaze of her lipstick on the glass threads burns when I taste it.

My phone keeps chiming. Dorothea's smile becomes more caustic with every
ding. I never charged the thing. I watch her snap a smug selfie and see that her
phone takes the same cable as mine.

"Let me see that," Andromeda says, when it becomes clear the chiming won't
stop. She swipes it open and frowns. "Wait, you have a date tonight? I thought
you said you weren't—oh. Gross." She doesn't turn the phone to show me, but
I can see enough of the screen to know it's not just an emoji this time. Dorothea
smiles again. Her teeth are so bleached they almost glow a superheated blue. "Oh,"
Andromeda says again. "You let him call you Val?"

When the doorbell rings, Dorothea is on her feet. "I'll get it," she says. She is
in the hall before I have a chance to say *please don't*. I think about how Andromeda and I always use the same screen lock pattern. I wonder how careful she is
about swiping into her phone around Dorothea. I wonder what Kevin read that
encouraged him so much. I know it wasn't something I sent.

My legs radiate heat like smouldering fuses. I cower closer to Luka. He's had a
lot of chances, and he's never taken them. He's been helping me home all week.
He's never too busy. I know it's for Andromeda's sake, or maybe it's solidarity,

but still. I brace my hand on his solid thigh to push myself upright. He does not flinch at the squishing of my fingers.

Dorothea's alkaline smile widens as she ushers Kevin into the room. I wonder why she hates me so much. Andromeda has so many others. We can never bear to let her go, even after she forgets. My hand smears across Luka's creased wool slacks and I am so sorry because I have never seen him stained. The room is wavering in the heat and I know I never told Kevin where I live. He walks toward me and Luka stands up and I want to hide behind him because I know he understands enough to know why there will never be anyone else for me.

Andromeda is shouting from the bathroom. I hear the faucets burst on like opened sluice gates. "Luka, help me get her into the bath. Cold water, the cold will make everything okay. Everything is going to be okay." It sounds like a prayer.

They try to lower me into the swelling seas as gently as a lifeboat. I am dripping between their hands and no one took the bottle cap from Andromeda's last shower out from under the treacherous stopper. Whatever burns in my veins is all I am.

I need it out. I need me out.

Dorothea smiles from the doorway. Luka pushes her aside. Andromeda is yelling at him to fetch all the ice in the world. The water forms a whirlpool, swirling me down. Andromeda's fingertips slip on the slick cap. The drain is inescapably close. The water in my mouth is brackish with residue from the salts we use in the bath. The tide rushes out the open porthole and I follow.

These Small Violences

J.A.W. McCarthy

E very time we did it, we punished ourselves:

Holding hands meant a pinch on the arm.

An arm around the shoulders warranted an elbow to the ribs.

A hug—whether he was comforting me or celebrating an A in Pre-Biology—was punished with an open-handed smack.

And a kiss—that was a fist to the face.

These small violences were no deterrent. Pleasure stayed pleasure, and pain, the climax of that pleasure. Every smack and slap and punch took a piece of us, buried that bit of our youth in its own place and time as we stumbled and panted and grinned through the pain.

The last time, I hit him so hard he disappeared.

———◦———

Though the landlord has painted over the wall where I sprayed Robby's blood fifteen years ago, I know this is the right spot.

Drywall dust clouds my vision, the last puff coating my face and hands as I finish with the jab saw and pop out the small square of wall. The underside is marred by black spores arranged in a loose orb, a cone of breath from the startled O of Robby's mouth that burrowed through the paint, leaving a stain uniquely his.

He laughed. I remember that. Standing in this room—his room, when we were eleven—he kissed me again and I punched him again until we were both bent over, hands on knees, laughing so hard we couldn't breathe.

When I would kiss him, his punch was noncommittal, my cheek molding gently around his knuckles, a little spit on my lower lip but not enough blood to outline my teeth.

I use a utility knife to scrape the black spores from the drywall square. The sticky blooms cling to each other, naked and vulnerable, frightened like we should've been when we were kids. Musty odors rise as I coax the spores into the little glass jar where I've been collecting Robby's remains. PlayDoh and cheap body spray, the smell of a kid trying to be a man.

"What are you doing?"

A woman stands in the doorway, hands braced on either side of the frame, her expression set in a series of lines that have not yet hardened beyond skepticism. I can work with this.

"You have mold," I tell her, holding up the piece of drywall. I trace my finger around the smeared stain the spores have left behind.

"What are you doing in my daughter's bedroom? Why would you—? You cut into my wall?"

The panic's rising now, cracking her face as her wide eyes narrow. Her hand slides from the doorframe to her back pocket, 9-1-1 surely unspooling in her mind.

"I smelled mold," I say calmly, firmly. I meet her eyes so she can see I'm confident, unashamed. "Your landlord sent me to check."

Her mouth twitches, but her shoulders relax. She unhooks her hand from her back pocket. "I thought you said you were here to check the furnace."

"Your landlord didn't want to worry you, in case it wasn't mold."

"Why does he think there's mold?"

"He ... Mr. ..."

"Anderson," she finishes.

"Mr. Anderson is getting insurance quotes for all his properties. He wanted to get ahead of the inspectors."

She nods, refocusing on the small drywall square I'm holding. Though I'm a stranger breaching the sanctity of this woman's home, the fear of dangerous mold threatening her child's health is stronger than any wariness over a baby-faced young woman lying about furnace maintenance.

"So, what happens next?" she asks, fresh concern lacing her words.

I place the drywall sample and jab saw in my bag. "I'll take this to show Mr. Anderson, then he'll send an abatement crew over. He'll call you."

With a reassuring smile I brush past her and head down the stairs. She even thanks me as I leave. I just cut open her wall, left a mess of paint flakes and drywall dust, and she thanks *me*. Where's the fun in that?

"What will our neighbors think?" my mother would ask when I wanted Robby to come over.

My father was blunter: "We don't associate with those people."

Robby's family lived in the apartments across the park. According to my parents, that building was full of single mothers and unattended children, addicts and criminals. I wasn't allowed to go over there because his recently-released brother sometimes stayed there too, and his mother couldn't be trusted when she spent her days doped up on pills. Not only was it unsafe, my parents insisted, but it would mark me, as if their degeneracy would tarnish the thin veneer of legitimacy my parents had worked so hard to cultivate. After years of double shifts and working towards a perfect credit score, my parents had finally moved us to the good part of town. Those apartments across the park were an insult to people like us, people who did everything they could to avoid taking government handouts.

Robby and I first met in the park, two eleven-year-olds trying to prolong those magical hours after school and before dinner. We'd sit in the grass reading comic books and ride our bikes as far as we could peddle. He came and went as he pleased and stayed up as late as he wanted.

His mother didn't frown at my presence, didn't ask me if my parents knew where I was, didn't gently suggest I befriend the kids who lived on the other side of the street. She hugged her son and called him "honey" right in front me, public expressions of affection my parents found improper. I envied Robby.

"My parents found out I come here after school. They said I can't anymore," I told him one afternoon. We were in his room, him on the bed and me on the floor, tossing a beanbag back and forth.

"Is it because you're rich?" he asked, catching the bag in one hand.

"We're not rich. My parents are liars. They're fake."

He gestured at my navy sweater vest and plaid skirt. "You go to that fancy school. Are you a scholarship kid?"

My parents had applied for scholarships for me, but only the academic ones; none of their friends' kids needed financial assistance. Really, it felt more like another thing to hold over my head: How dare I waste my time with someone like Robby when they had sacrificed so much for me to have a superior education?

"No," I answered.

He hurled the bean bag against the opposite wall, knocking a book from the shelf there. "So you are rich. Or pretend rich. Too good to hang out with me anyway."

"I don't want to talk about this anymore. Wanna kiss?"

Robby never said no when I asked.

It wasn't that we were *in* love. He was my best friend because he liked *The Sandman* too, and he didn't think I was gross because *Dead Alive* was my favorite movie. He didn't care that my shoes were plastic instead of patent leather, or that I wore the same shirt every day, not like the kids at my school did.

We'd been holding hands lately, sometimes when we walked through the park, or during the scary parts of the videos we watched in his living room—that was worth the pinches we administered, payment for the small comfort I wasn't getting at home. The kissing was new, though. We tried it, then kept doing it because it felt nice and seemed like something we'd need to get good at one day. The punishment for that had to be as heavy as the blanket of guilt that would be waiting for me when I got home. Pleasure became rebellion became shame I had to scrub off until my lips bled.

We both had to bleed.

So we kissed right there in his room, Robby leaning over the edge of the bed to meet me on the floor. It was wet and quick. He tasted like Cheetos and spearmint gum.

When we parted, he looked as excited as I felt. "Okay," he said, standing up with me. "I'm ready."

He squeezed his eyes shut and I punched him, my clumsy fist landing on the corner of his mouth. It was hard enough this time to spray a thin mist of blood onto the wall.

After the initial shock, he grinned and started laughing. We laughed together until we were both doubled over and panting, me rubbing my aching knuckles, Robby with pink drool running down his chin. Then he kissed me again and I punched him again. When it was time for his fist to meet my cheek, he was gentler than I was, careful to not leave marks my parents would see. The pain made me feel held, important. I wanted it again and again, more than anything.

⸻◆⸻

Fifteen years ago, this building was Newberry Drugs, abandoned first by the business owners, then the kids who would get high and graffiti the cleaned-out space. Robby and I would sneak in when it was too rainy to go to the park, gorging on Abba-Zabbas and failing at kickflips on his skateboard. We might've bled the most here.

Now it's been remodeled into an advertising agency, all conflicting angles of metal, glass and cedar. There are a lot of people buzzing around the generous lobby, so I slip easily into the stream. Expensive shoes and laptop keys clack in a dual melody as people glide toward various glass-walled offices. Dashes of bright colors juxtapose with somber, slick suits, only a jewel-toned blouse or lapel pin to signal any creativity or individualism. The kind of place my parents wanted me to work.

I find an empty conference room and get started. The minimalist tables and chairs don't afford much privacy as I crouch behind them, reaching up to force my jab saw into the drywall. Robby and I sprayed our blood all over this place, so I should be able to get the spores easily. Every time, I'm calling to him, even if he has yet to answer. I don't know how else to reach him, but I won't stop trying. I will give him what he wants, what he needs.

As I'm making the last cut, a woman stops in the doorway, but averts her eyes and hurries away before I can say anything. I pop out the drywall square and admire the cross-section of cool grey over layers of white primer. Beneath that, a shock of electric green. Robby's blood had looked stunning splattered across the graffiti—the rich, saturated red bisecting the bright complimentary bubble letters.

A hug when Robby slammed and rolled his ankle. A kiss when I landed a tail slide. My fist hitting harder than I'd intended, blood and spit misting everywhere as his head tapped the wall. An "I'm sorry" kiss on the cheek, followed by a punch that left me rubbing my chin all afternoon.

I'm scraping the black spores from the back when I look up to see a man in the doorway.

"What's going on here?"

I shift so that I'm blocking the hole I've made. "Oh, are you Mr. Sutherland? I'm supposed to—" I force a nervous laugh. "They told me to wait for him here, but it's been a long time."

The man narrows his eyes. "Did you just cut into the wall?"

"The agency told me Mr. Sutherland would meet me, get me oriented and started on my assignment."

"Which agency? What are you here to do?"

"I'm the new temp." I keep my voice buoyant. I have to remain both convinced and convincing, any doubt not my own. "For your AP department."

"No one told me about that. We don't need anyone there."

This is the part where I would leave, but he's blocking the doorway, shoulders stretching the limit of his shiny grey suit as he crosses his arms. He surveys me from head to toe, pausing at the chunk of wall still in my hands. I won't be able to explain this one, and it looks like it'll hurt when he tosses me out.

"Oh, god, I've messed up again, haven't I?" The tears come easily; all I have to do is think about Robby. "This is McCullough & Sons, isn't it? I've already been late twice this month—I'm so bad with directions. The agency said if I messed up again, they'd drop me." I gasp for breath, resisting the urge to wipe away the tears tickling my jawline. "Oh god, if I don't make rent this month—"

The man's eyes linger on the square of wall in my hand, then skim my white dust-coated shoulders and sleeves, and I have to squash the urge to preen in my ill-fitting blazer. I'm ugly-crying now, mascara streaks and all. It works because I'm a woman and I look young; when I play that up, people often want to take care of me, give me what they think I need even if they're not usually the type to take such a risk for a stranger.

"Oh, geez. Okay, okay." He moves towards me, extending a hand then pulling back when I let out a whimper. "McCullough & Sons is just down the block. You can still get there," he says, voice softening. "Why don't you go get, uh, cleaned up in the restroom and I'll bring you a cup of coffee. How's that sound?"

"That's so kind. Thank you so much."

I'm out of there the minute he heads down the hall.

———◆———

Bringing Robby to my house was the ultimate rebellion. The one time I had him over before, my parents treated him the same as any of my other friends—my mother offering cookies and my dad a ride home after dinner—until they started asking questions. What did his parents do for a living? What school did he go to? Where did he live? Their faces twitched, straining to maintain those approving smiles.

When Robby mentioned his formerly incarcerated brother, it was suddenly past my bedtime, and Robby's too.

There'd been hand-wringing, my parents worrying if they were doing the right thing about a "disadvantaged" child like Robby. Perhaps I could be a good influence on him, our home a safe haven where he could enjoy balanced meals at the solid oak dining set my parents had finally finished paying off. Then they started talking about the what-ifs, my dad worrying that Robby could get me pregnant and ruin my life even though we were only eleven. Soon, he wasn't allowed in our house at all.

So Robby was surprised when one rainy afternoon I invited him over. My parents would both be home from work soon. I was vibrating with the anticipation of our punishment ritual, how my fist would feel against his jaw, his knuckles against my lips.

"What will your mom do if she finds ... a *smudge*?" he asked, splaying out on the couch. He lifted his legs so that his mud-spattered sneakers hovered in the air, threatening the matching ottoman.

"You wouldn't."

He lowered his legs, his heels almost kissing the white brocade.

"Don't."

He raised then abruptly dropped his feet again.

"Don't you dare!" I squealed, diving onto the couch. He swung his feet away and onto the floor before I could catch them. "My mom," I said.

"Your mom what? What would she do if I—" He raised his hands, wiggling his fingers in my face, "—*touched* everything with my *filthy* fingers?"

I pushed his hands away. "Why are you being like this?"

"Why do you want me here? If you can't come to my place, that means I can't be here either." He looked down at his hands. His knuckles were scraped from my teeth the last time he hit me. "I know what your parents say about me," he said. "My brother's a fuckup, sure, but my mom ... she got hurt real bad at her last job, okay? That's why she can't work anymore. She takes those pills because she's always in pain."

I'd mentioned to my parents that Robby's mom didn't have a job, and I might've told them about the pills, too. I couldn't help myself from letting slip details they'd find unseemly, all for the thrill of pushing boundaries, of seeing their faces pinch with disdain.

"My parents are phonies," I told him. "They think everyone who's not their rich friends are trash."

"Just because I'm poor doesn't mean I'm trash."

"I didn't say you were trash. Robby!" I leaned close, but he turned away from me. "Robby, c'mon. Who cares what they say? When we grow up, we'll move to the city. No one there will care if we're rich or poor."

"It'll always matter."

I knew Robby was right. I could see it in the way my parents' friends spoke about "the unfortunates" in the city, the way my father's boss regarded our modest home with amusement when he came over for dinner. My family was pretending, barely keeping up appearances, and everyone could tell.

"I'm gonna go home," Robby said, rising. So I stood too, and I kissed him. My lips glanced his as he turned, leaving a shiny smear from the corner of his mouth to his cheek. He froze. I braced myself for the smack, a grin flinching on my lips, my fists already balling at my sides.

But he just stood there.

"C'mon!" I yelled when he still wouldn't move. My whole body prickled, all this energy pressing against my chest and my knees and my palms. "Do it!"

He tried to push past me towards the front door, but I blocked his way. Irritation tightened his face, made his eyes small and dark. I wanted him to react. So I grabbed his shoulders and kissed him again.

This time, he gave me the worst look. Like I was trash.

I hauled back and punched him the hardest I'd ever dared.

Blood from his nose and mouth sprayed the wall behind the couch. He didn't look shocked, even as he cupped the side of his face and his tongue darted out to test the blood that was accumulating on his upper lip. My knuckles split, revealing the bright pink, sticky flesh beneath. A drop of my own blood marred the white couch cushion, but that wasn't why I was scared. Robby was so still, so unreadable, I was sure I'd gone too far and he would never speak to me again.

Then he dropped his hand from his face and punched me back.

We went back and forth, punching and slapping each other, giddy, as blood stained our teeth and coated our tongues. I was floating with adrenaline, exhilarated by the warm throb rising along my jaw and under my eye even though I knew this time there would be bruises I couldn't hide. Robby was all over this house now, and I relished the thought of my mother scrubbing at our bloodstains, anxious with worry over who might see and what they might think.

"What will the neighbors think?" I shouted.

We were laughing so hard we didn't hear the front door open.

Before I knew it, Robby was being yanked backwards, his knuckles barely kissing my already numbing cheek. I pitched forward, aching for the contact, but then I noticed my dad with his hand wrapped around the back of Robby's neck.

"Get the hell out of my house and don't you ever touch my daughter again!" he screamed, dragging Robby across the room and to the open front door.

Robby's heels caught on the carpet, leaving a dark smudge on the beige expanse. "I knew it. You piece of shit," my dad growled. With a grunt, he tossed Robby onto the front porch and glared down at him splayed there and shaking. "If I ever see you around here, if I even hear my daughter say your name—" He didn't finish. The slam of the front door was the only punctuation he needed.

Any thrill I felt turned quickly to shame.

I really had gone too far this time. I'd punched Robby as hard as I ever had, and now I'd never see him again.

———◦———

I perch on the edge of the white brocade sofa, feeling out of place in my childhood home. Everything is as bright and flawless as it was fifteen years ago. If only I'd shown up with dirty hands, mud or sweat stains ready to blemish all this polished brass and glass and fabric. I remember the bruises on my jaw and under my eye from Robby's last punches and how my parents had fretted. How my mother's fingers lingered as she gently rubbed various balms on my wounds, an unfamiliar touch that I craved. Concern knitted her brow as she called me "sweetheart" and tut-tutted "that terrible boy," but I knew it had been all about one thing: *What will our neighbors think?*

Now, my mother's in the kitchen making tea. It's been almost two years since my last visit. I'm being treated like a guest, perhaps unwanted but welcome.

"Soon," I whisper to the wall behind me. I run my fingers over the eggshell paint. My parents only think they got rid of him.

I want to say that Robby never made it home that day. I want to say that his mother came to our house in tears, that we were interviewed by the police, that hundreds of flyers with his face were plastered all over town. I want to say that our neighbors saw my dad slam him down onto the porch that afternoon and everyone realized how phony my parents were.

Maybe I craved that kind of terrible drama because it was easier to accept than Robby's hatred. All I had left was the bone-deep ache of missing his hand, missing him. This wasn't the kind of pain I craved.

This is what happened: my parents told Robby's mom that they'd caught him hitting me. They threatened her, called her family trash, weaponized all the names that had once been hurled at us. Robby was there, in his room. He heard everything.

A week later, he left to live with his dad across the country.

I found that out when I talked to his mother. She refused when I asked for his number. At home, I cried until my parents made it clear I'd never leave my room again if I so much as said his name. My mother scrubbed the couch, then the wall hard enough to make a bald spot. My father repainted the entire living room. When I started talking to the wall where I'd sprayed Robby's blood, they pretended not to notice.

What I've been doing—going to the places where we bled, collecting the spores born from Robby's blood—used to be about bringing Robby back, a way to call him to me since he's ignored all of my messages. I can't be sure the Robby I found online is the same one I knew when we were eleven, but I know he will find me and he will answer if I get this right. It took a long time, but I finally figured out that what he needs is revenge.

"I'm sorry it's taken me so long," I say, stroking the wall. "I've been a coward."

My mother brings out her cloisonne tea set on a silver tray. The good stuff. She sets everything up on the coffee table instead of making me sit in the kitchen. I truly am a guest.

"Your father will be home soon," she says, pouring. "You'll stay for dinner?"

"Of course."

This brings a rare smile of approval to her face. I relish ruining it.

"You remember what happened to Robby?" I ask.

Her brow knits, but she keeps her focus on the stream of tea flowing neatly into my cup. "You should go wash your hands. I wasn't going to say anything, but I noticed you have some dust or something on your blazer."

"Did you ever talk to his mom? She missed him so much."

"Mmm ... sad," my mother mutters, pushing the cup towards me.

"He was my best friend and you always treated him ... Dad threw him out like he was fucking garbage."

She winces at my swearing.

"It wasn't his fault," I continue. "*I'm* the one who started the game. *I* punched him. I *wanted* him to punch me. You both acted like he would ruin my life, like he was a criminal just because he was poor. But we were poor, too. 'What will people think?' You think they didn't know? You think they didn't look down on us like we were pathetic trying to pretend?"

My mother takes a sip of her tea then sets the cup gently on the coffee table. How I long for her to slam that cup down instead, send porcelain and rooibos flying. Give me a reason to rethink my plan. Instead, her face remains still, composed.

"Stop this, right now. I don't want to hear about that boy anymore. Your father and I did everything we could to make sure you'd have a good life. If you'd kept associating with people like that—"

"What? I'd be in jail? Pregnant? Because that's all 'those people' do, right? Fight and fuck?"

She winces again. "Why do you have to be like this? I was so happy to see you," she says, her voice wavering as she rises from her seat. For the briefest second, it looks like I'll get what I want: tears, a raised voice, an outpouring of raw, unrestrained emotion. Maybe she'll slap me, or hug me—I don't care which. But it's a fleeting moment, her composure seamlessly resuming as she brushes the creases from her slacks. "I don't know why you insist on digging up the past."

I sip my tea, disappointment failing to dampen the familiar thrill rising in my chest. "You're right. I'm sorry. Do you have any cream?"

"Cream? I'll have to look."

While she's in the kitchen, I grab the little glass jar I've been using to collect Robby's remains and tip some of the black spores out into her cup. The faint scent of PlayDoh blooms in the air, then fades as I stir. I'm tempted to take a sip—or better yet, dip the tip of my tongue into that jar and coax out a single spore for myself—but maybe I'm better off with my memories of Cheeto salt and copper on his lips.

My mother returns with a ceramic creamer. I pour a little into my tea and stir, watching as she sips from her own cup. I wait for her to react, to comment on the strange musty or coppery or salty flavor, but she keeps sipping as if that cup is the only thing sustaining her poised facade.

She's still clutching it when her eyes go wide.

The cup crashes against the coffee table, brass cleaving porcelain into pieces that bounce off the carpet. This might be the most satisfying moment of my life. The scandal of the good china not only dropped but broken, brown liquid staining the carpet, my mother clutching her throat while her other hand flails to acknowledge the mess. I wasn't sure any of this would happen, but now that it is, I see Robby again. Everywhere. Answering me.

Once my mother goes quiet—face down on the floor, fingers stretching towards the remnants of her cup—I get out my jab saw and go to work on the wall behind the couch. Dust floods my nostrils as I saw, then the familiar mustiness once I pop out the piece of wall. My mouth goes dry, gums shriveling, the sen-sation of ash on my tongue even though I won't allow myself a taste. I quickly scrape the spores into the little jar. This is it. The last of Robby.

Dad will be home soon.

The Dust Collectors

Shenoa Carroll-Bradd

N ancy found The Dust Collectors' card taped to her front door and pulled it off with a frown. What a strange thing to call a cleaning service. *Chemical free*, it boasted. She would have dropped the little rectangle into the recycling bin if not for a familiar scrawl in ballpoint along the bottom.

Recommended by: Cynthia Green

She brought it in with the morning newspaper, setting both aside while she turned her attention to making coffee. She certainly had fallen behind in her cleaning—never developed a taste for the chore—and the new year was coming up. Time for new habits and fresh starts. Had she mentioned her hatred of housekeeping to Cynthia? She must have. They talked about everything, and Cyn was a champion listener. If Nancy had complained even once, she'd been heard.

While the coffee brewed, she pulled out her phone and snapped a picture of the card, framed by the dingy blue tile of her kitchen island.

—Got your recommendation for a cleaning service. You like these guys?

Her message clicked over from delivered to read and then remained there so long, Nancy assumed she'd been forgotten. She was halfway through her first cup when Cynthia replied.

—They're thorough.

Nancy waited for more, watching the bottom of the screen for those three dots to appear, but nothing came.

Odd. Cyn was the type of texter who sent three messages, rapid fire, when a single line would suffice.

Nancy shrugged and went back to her day. But as she moved about the house, it seemed like everywhere she looked bore a grey patina of dust and grime, until the whole place suddenly felt filthy. Shocking how invisible neglect could become if it was routine enough. Just another downside to living alone. Someone else's mess she'd be certain to notice, and another pair of hands picking up the place would help. But, left to her own devices, a cozy level of slovenliness had crept in. Nancy returned to the kitchen and considered the card.

New year, new habits. New hope.

———◇———

At precisely the time she'd selected from The Dust Collectors' automated system, they arrived at her door. A little strange not speaking directly to anyone, but that was just how the world worked these days. Everything automated, everyone so busy they had no time left to chat.

The men at her door immediately gave her pause. Three of them stood on her doorstep, all pale, all bald. All looking ever-so-slightly sick, like they'd been denied vegetables and sunlight since childhood. Each wore a dark, stiff suit, like an undertaker drawn in triplicate. The tallest one smiled in a way that made Nancy run her tongue over her own teeth, just to check their proper number and shape.

"Madam called for cleaners," he said.

Not a question, and not spoken in a cadence she could place. She wasn't sure if it was an accent, or just unnervingly deliberate enunciation. Her hand tightened on the door. "You're the ... Dust Collectors?"

All three nodded, heads bobbing like a nest full of vultures.

Nancy swallowed her nerves. Well, they were here. She called and they came, and now it would be rude to turn them away just because their English wasn't perfect and they dressed a little odd. Besides, there was probably some sort of cancellation fee. Against the curling in her stomach, Nancy opened the door wider.

"Great. Thanks for coming."

The men filed past like strange ducklings, looking all around them. It put her in mind of schoolchildren at an art museum. Their heads swiveled about as if every inch of her home demanded their attention and they couldn't decide where to let their gazes rest.

"And how long do you think this will take?" Maybe she would pop out to the coffeeshop, or the grocery store. Go over and see Cynthia, maybe. Nancy wasn't exactly eager to leave her home in the hands of unsupervised strangers, even though she'd already taken the precaution of tucking any valuables out of sight. But on the other hand, staying put to watch them work sounded awkward and domineering.

"An hour," the tallest one said. Their spokesperson, apparently. Though as she noticed, they didn't wear nametags on their strange uniforms, making them hard to distinguish from one another.

"Really? Just an hour? And that's for the whole house?"

The other two kept up their rubbernecking inspection while the spokesman turned his full attention to her.

"Good teamwork, madam."

He delivered another smile that made her want to climb out of her skin before gesturing to where the sun shone on the porch swing, visible through the kitchen window. "Madam can wait outside with a book. We will only need a few chapters' time to do our work."

She felt her eyes pinch in what was almost a smile, though the top half and bottom of her face couldn't quite agree.

"Oh, okay. Sure, I can sit outside for a while."

His lips drew back, mirroring her expression.

Nancy turned away from the sight. She grabbed a half-finished beach read from where it sat abandoned on the counter, and escaped to her front porch. Only once the door closed behind her did the tension in her neck begin to ease.

She settled onto the porch swing with the book gripped two-handed in her lap. For a moment, she just sat there, staring out at the sunlit street. Everything looked so normal out here. She let the warmth soak into her skin, listened to the birdsong. Even the coughing growl of a nearby lawnmower sounded quotidian and sweet.

Setting the book aside, Nancy pulled out her phone and opened her last text to Cynthia.

—*Cleaners just got here. Kinda weird, aren't they?*

Read, but no response.

Cyn never did that to her. *Must be having a hell of a day.* Nancy could walk the block and a half to go see her in person, but that might just add one more stressor. *I'm sure I'll hear all about it tomorrow.*

She put her phone away, but couldn't bring herself to open the book. She didn't want to read, not really, and if she forced herself to try, Nancy knew she'd just end up rereading the same paragraph again and again for the next hour.

A spot between her shoulders itched. The warmth of the sun was now making her sweat.

How long had it been since she'd had strangers in her home? Especially without her there to supervise or play hostess? It felt ... wrong.

Plus, something had nagged at her from the moment the men arrived—something missing from the whole situation. Not only was there the absence of a branded van parked at the curb, but none of them carried vacuums, rags, or dusters of any kind. Her spine stiffened. What were they doing in there then, with no cleaning supplies?

She should have asked for their names, at least, or some form of ID before letting three strangers into her home. But she had been so eager to leave them to it.

Now she twisted to peer through the kitchen window behind her. All she saw was the glare of the day reflected back and the dark suggestion of her kitchen island, like a rock submerged in a murky stream. There was nothing for it. She'd have to go back inside if she wanted to observe them. The cleaners. The Dust Collectors. Why did that name make her so uneasy?

She rose from the porch swing and crept to her own front door, feeling like a trespasser. Nancy eased down the thumb latch and pushed it in gently, careful to stop before reaching the spot where it liked to squeak.

This was silly—this was her home!

And yet, she hated the thought of disturbing them, of seeing their pale heads whip around to face her like a clutch of startled snakes.

At first, Nancy didn't see the cleaners. Were they in her bedroom, fingering her delicates and hunting for what treasures she'd locked away?

Peeking around the corner of the foyer, she saw that no, they were performing no such invasion. All three were hard at work in the living room.

Nancy now understood why the dark-suited men brought no rags or cleaning supplies of their own.

They walked slowly about her house as if it were a museum, just like she'd first observed. They kept their hands respectfully folded behind their backs as they leaned close to whatever object caught their attention, and then—they licked it.

They opened pale jaws, revealing swollen, purple-red tongues that extended more than a foot, maybe even two, and seemed impossible to logically house within the structure of their throats and skulls. Their tongues lapped at the surface of everything she owned, digging up dust from crevices and needling it out of corners. They made no sound, but she felt the unspoken moans rippling through the air, underscored by the way their hands sporadically clutched and writhed by the base of their spines, like feral creatures barely held in place.

Nancy covered her mouth with one hand, not even wanting to breathe in the same room. Her entrance had been silent, and yet one of the Dust Collectors raised his gaze to hers and held it while his tongue continued its path along the edge of a magazine stack. If he had any fear of papercuts slicing the dark veins of that exposed organ, it did not show.

Nancy fled as quietly as she could. She returned to the porch swing, one leg bouncing as she clenched her hands between her knees. What could she do? Report them to the police? Get up and walk away, sell the house, start somewhere new? Every solution seemed so frail in the shadow of that red and writhing tongue. That impossible organ, laving over each piece of the life she'd built.

Finally, the front door creaked open.

Her leg stopped bouncing. Nancy held her neck stiff, not daring to look over, terrified that she might see their three bald heads peering around the threshold, a cadaverous totem pole.

"Madam," the familiar voice crooned. "We have finished cleaning."

Nancy rose and marched into her home, joints rigid, jaw tight. Calling them had been a mistake. She'd tell them to leave, right now, and she didn't appreciate ...

Her steps faltered as she came around the foyer. Her house was so spotless it shone. She raised a hand halfway to her eyes before catching herself. It hadn't been this clean when she moved in. It probably hadn't even been this clean when it was first built.

They'd cleaned not only the surface dust, but stripped off the age, the wear, the fading. The place was better than pristine. It was perfect.

The Dust Collectors stood to the side, hands behind their backs, as always, but now with a hint of what might have been pride on their alien faces.

Nancy hurried to fetch her purse from the kitchen, keeping the jewel-like island between herself and them. She wrote out a check with numb fingers and pushed it across.

The lead cleaner tilted his head, looked at it a moment, then drew a business card from inside his jacket and set it beside the check.

It was identical to the one she'd found on her door, only without the blue ink scrawl at the bottom.

"Madam will recommend us to a friend."

She shook her head, barely stifling a disgusted laugh. They'd performed a service and she'd pay them for their time, but no, she would not inflict this on anyone else ...

The lead cleaner bowed his head closer.

This near, Nancy could see blue veins squiggle beneath his skin, like strange marble or strong cheese. It made her stomach turn.

"Madam will recommend a friend," he repeated solemnly, "or our service will return weekly."

Nancy's fingers took the card before she registered what she was doing. No wonder Cynthia refused to talk to her today. Her best friend had saddled her with a curse, the deceitful cow.

"Emily Ann-Jones," she said quickly, writing the address on the back of the offered card, then flipping it over to sign her name on the referred by line. She shoved it in his direction.

The Dust Collector retrieved his card with long, knuckle-less fingers and tucked it back inside his jacket. "Madam has made a wise choice."

Then the three turned and silently shuffled out of the house.

They'd left the check behind, but Nancy didn't care as she rushed to close the door behind them. No vehicle arrived to collect them, and when she craned her neck, their dark shapes were nowhere to be seen along the sunny street. With a shiver, she slammed and locked the door.

Looking down at the sparkling handle in her grip, Nancy recoiled. That sheen. That almost imperceptible shellac covering everything. How much had she already touched? She wrapped her arms around herself, squeezing, but not giving comfort. As she turned to take in her immaculate home, Nancy ground her sullied fingertips into the fabric of her shirt. Her house had never been so perfect. And she had never been so eager to leave it. Every surface now shone with an invisible, unforgettable stain.

One usually associated pine and lemon scents with cleanliness, the artificial signs of freshness. But there was none of that here.

Chemical-free, her home smelled only of violation.

The World of Iniquity Among Our Members is the Tongue

D. Matthew Urban

A melia Strutt showed up to Haystown High School one September morning wearing a mask. It was a shapely wooden thing with a delicate nose and a high forehead that rose past the edge of her dark curls, its eyes two white discs of birch bark with little holes to see through. A band of red elastic around the back of Amelia's head held the mask tight to her face. There was no mouth.

If anyone else had worn a mask to school, they would have been taunted, jostled—at the very least giggled at, but Amelia was granted certain immunities. Her mother had died the previous summer—killed in a car crash—and the disaster's magnitude bestowed an almost superhuman stature on the sixteen-year-old survivor.

"James," my own mother had said to me upon hearing the news, pale and large-eyed, phone shaking in her hand, "Amelia Strutt has lost her mother." I pictured Mrs. Strutt slipping like a stray glove from her daughter's pocket to vanish on some dark wayside.

The fact that Amelia's father was a minister, associate pastor at Haystown United Methodist, never seemed particularly important, least of all to Amelia. After his wife's death, though, a change came over Rev. Strutt, as if a bitter wind had driven him into the shelter of his own darkness. Once a friendly, laughing, almost foolish man, he now sat scowling every Sunday in his chair beneath the pulpit, hands clenched in his lap, eyes furiously ablaze, and the sight of him reminded me that *reverend*, as my bookish aunt Stacy once told me, means *fearsome*. Her father's newfound zeal cast a strange glare on Amelia, set her further apart from the rest of us. Daughter of death and terrible holiness, swept away by a storm from another world.

For the first few weeks of that semester, our sense of Amelia's separation drove us to acts of inordinate politeness. When she dropped her tray in the cafeteria, no one laughed. When a book fell from her arms in the hall, a dozen hands reached to pick it up. Doors opened for her, chairs slid back from library tables to offer themselves. "Good to see you, Amelia," we'd simper through strychnine smiles. "See you tomorrow, Amelia." "Have a great weekend, Amelia." She drifted among our courtesies with dull eyes and vague gestures, a drowned girl floating on a tide of meaningless words.

Then, the mask.

I heard about Amelia's mask before I saw it, vague accounts rippling in awed whispers through the halls, so when I stepped into Mrs. Lagrange's precalculus class and saw Amelia sitting at her front-row desk, red elastic stretched like a slashed throat across the back of her skull, just the thought of that wooden face filled me with dread. White eyes swelled and throbbed in my imagination like jellyfish, a phantom mouth, gaping invisibly. I gripped the jamb of the classroom door with trembling fingers to keep from swooning.

After a moment, my terror receded, humiliation boiling in its wake. *You baby*, I told myself. *It's just a mask.* I strode to the front of the class and sat down at the desk next to Amelia's.

The mask swiveled toward me. Through the holes in its flat, round eyes I glimpsed the shimmer and movement of real eyes. From behind the smooth wood, I heard the faint rustle of breath echoing in a narrow space. Licking my dry lips, I attempted to speak.

The bell clanged.

The mask turned away.

Mrs. Lagrange rose from her paper-strewn desk to drone about the zeros of polynomial curves, but in my mind, the zeros paled into white circles of bark set in the gentle curve of a false face, hidden things glinting and darting behind them like terrible questions veiled behind smiles. *What is it like,* I whispered in my mind, *to be you?* I felt my mouth vanish, my eyes diminish to pinpricks. I put my head down on the desk.

The next thing I felt was Mrs. Lagrange's hand on my shoulder.

"Are you all right, James?" she asked.

"I'm great," I said.

"You look pale," she said. "Why don't you go see the nurse."

I lay on a cot in the nurse's office until the bell rang for lunch.

———◦———

In the cafeteria, my friends were in our usual spot, hunched over the table and murmuring among themselves. Their murmurs faded when I set my tray down in the middle of the group. Everyone's eyes slid away from mine.

"What's the big secret?" I said.

"Dude," said Brian. "Did you say something to Amelia before class?"

"No, man. I didn't say a word to her."

Thomas glared at me from across the table. "Well, I heard you were making fun of her. I heard you got sent to the principal's office like a fucking kindergartner."

"Who the hell told you that? I went to the nurse. I was feeling sick."

Susan leaned toward me, her eyes flashing. "I talked to someone who's in Mrs. Lagrange's class with you, and she said you were acting like you were scared of ..." She glanced around before lowering her voice to a whisper. "Like you were scared of Amelia's mask. Like it made you sick. She said you were hamming it up, being a real asshole."

"I wasn't ..." I broke off, snarling with frustration, my breath hot in my throat. What could I say to defend myself? *I wasn't acting, I really was scared? Scared of the mask? Scared I* was *the mask?* They'd still think I was making fun of Amelia, keeping the cruel joke alive. And if they didn't think that—if they knew I was serious, that I'd truly been terrified—and they were just pretending I'd been joking, acting as if I'd been acting, veil behind veil, mask over mask over mask ...

I shook my head clear. "So what?" I said. I looked across the cafeteria to the corner table where Amelia sat alone, no tray in front of her, masked.

"Should I go apologize?"

"Yes, asshole," said Brian. "You should apologize."

"Apologize," said Susan.

"Apologize, asshole," said Thomas.

"Fine." I pushed my chair back with a scoff.

My eyes stayed fixed on the red slash across the back of Amelia's head as I walked to the corner table. I thought about how, when someone dies in a movie or a TV show, the family has to identify the body. *Does that happen in real life?* I envisioned Amelia standing over her mother's corpse, a broken thing on a metal slab. I'd seen Mrs. Strutt at church and school functions, spoken to her a few times. I could remember what she looked like, but the face in my memory was only a veil, a mask over the real face I pictured Amelia seeing on that slab—a ruined and violated mass of flesh I couldn't even bear to imagine. It felt somehow indecent, discourteous toward the dead, to want to catch a glimpse of that real face.

I stood behind Amelia's chair wondering how long I'd been there. Blushing with shame, I cleared my throat. "Amelia?"

The white circles beheld me, and the eyes behind them beheld the circles beholding me. The delicate nose—*more delicate than Amelia's*, I thought, and the thought made me feel so guilty I wanted to cut my throat, slash myself open to spill an endless red apology ...

The delicate nose seemed to quiver. Breath echoed inside the mask, sliding along the hidden face.

"Amelia," I said. "I wanted to apolo..."

A startled gasp I couldn't contain cut the word in half. Amelia was gesturing wildly, waving her hands back and forth in front of her, swinging her head sharply side to side. *No, no, no,* her frantic movement said.

As I stood in astonished silence, Amelia reached into a pocket of her jacket and pulled out a three-by-five notecard. She scrawled on the card in ballpoint pen, folded it into thirds and handed it to me. When I reached for it, she lifted her other hand to the mask, to the smooth space where there was no mouth. With the tips of her fingers, she traced the curve of a smile over the wood.

I didn't dare say "Thank you," but felt I had to do something to show my appreciation. Some mark of courtesy to keep the mask in place, hold the veil secure against the terrible storm. So, I bowed awkwardly, like I'd seen servants do in movies. Then, I hurried back to my table, my friends.

"Way to go," said Brian.

"That was really nice of you," said Susan.

I unfolded the top flap of the card.

JAMES, it said. As if a mask had fallen away to reveal my own face, my own name floating from behind a veil in taunting singsong, *Ja-ames, Ja-ames.* I choked. Coughed. Blinked away tears.

Brian thumped me on the back. "Dude, you all right?"

"I'm fine. Down the wrong pipe."

Next, the second flap of the card.

JAMES 3:6. Not me, James Helmholtz, but James 3:6. A second mask had fallen away—my own mask-face dropping to show another face—the scowling Rev. Strutt, sitting below the pulpit with eyes that flared like coals.

"Hey, Thomas," I said. "You got your Bible?" Thomas's parents were Church of Christ weirdos who made him bring a Bible to school every day. He fished it out of his backpack.

Letter of James, chapter 3, verse 6: *And the tongue is a fire: the world of iniquity among our members is the tongue, which defileth the whole body, and setteth on fire the wheel of nature, and is set on fire by hell.*

I gave Thomas back his Bible and refolded the card to put in my pocket. As I finished my lunch, I pictured a faceless girl drifting down a hallway, floating through a kelp forest where creatures flitted between thick vegetal strands, slimy ragged tongues, words bubbling from behind their masks in vile, oily clouds—*Good to see you. Good to see you. Good to see you.*

———◆———

What I'd learned in the cafeteria that day, everyone else seemed to realize by instinct. The mask was not to be addressed in words, only acknowledged in feats of increasing politeness, ever more abject deference. The mask was a third step away from us, beyond a dead mother and a fanatic father into some realm so distant, only the broadest, most blatant gestures could reach it.

As Amelia walked through the halls, the other students parted before her like human curtains. Football players fell to their knees as she passed, cheerleaders curtsied in their pleated skirts, AV club members grinned and gave her two thumbs up.

The mask accepted it all with a nod, cold and majestic as the Queen of Silence.

No one ever saw Amelia outside of school anymore. Susan said a friend of hers who lived across the street from the Strutts had caught a glimpse of the mask in a second-floor window, gazing out over the street. When Susan's friend saw those birch-bark circles looking down at her, that delicate nose and missing mouth, she threw herself on the ground, covered her head with her arms and wriggled on the ground like the worm she was.

"It was all she could think to do," said Susan. "She had to show respect somehow."

———◆———

Every Sunday, as my mother and I drove to Haystown United Methodist, I trembled with dread and anticipation, wondering if this would be the time Amelia came to watch her father pray. She never attended service, so instead of staring transfixed and abased at the mask, I observed the changes in Rev. Strutt.

His furious intensity grew week by week, and as it blazed higher, I felt ever more convinced that his spiritual devotion was a disguise, a mask. I could see something else at work through its holes—something quick and shining: fear. Behind his fanatical facade, Rev. Strutt was utterly terrified.

To my surprise, when I mentioned this revelation to my mother, she agreed right away.

"Of course he's afraid," she said. "His life is falling apart. We all see it. When I meet up with folks from church, it's all anyone talks about. We all wish there was something we could do."

Emboldened by her openness, I said, "Well, maybe there is. Have you asked him if he needs help?"

"Just come right out and ask?" She side-eyed me over the driver's seat. "That would be a little tacky, don't you think? The poor man's flailing already, wouldn't want to make him feel worse by letting him know we know."

The next Monday, Amelia fell while getting up from her desk when the bell rang at the end of Mrs. Lagrange's class. Nobody saw her fall—by that time, everyone in school had tacitly agreed it would be rude to watch Amelia get up and leave a room, or walk down a hall, or travel from place to place in any way. We couldn't treat her like any ordinary person who had to move through space to get from Point A to Point B. This was Amelia, after all.

We'd sit at our desks—leaving hers empty like a robbed grave—and close our eyes until we heard Amelia's slow, steady steps cross the room; the quiet creaking of her desk as she sat; the shuffling of papers in her backpack. Then, we'd open our eyes, and it would be as if she'd appeared out of thin air. At the end of class, we'd close our eyes again until her steps had faded into the hallway outside.

That day, though, instead of the sound of Amelia rising and leaving, there was a heavy shifting of the desk—metal legs scraping tile, a swish of cloth, and a scrabbling of hands against wood. The thump of a falling body. Stillness.

Nobody moved.

After that, all we heard was a faint, rustling slide of trapped air. Breath haunting the space behind the mask.

I couldn't help but peek, glanced around the room. Everyone else still had their eyes shut, locked in courteous oblivion. I turned to where Amelia lay between the front row of desks and the blackboard, her arms feebly circling as if she were trying to swim across the floor.

It had been weeks since I'd dared to look closely at her, and I was shocked at how thin her limbs were, how slow and clumsy her movements. *How long since she's eaten?* Beneath the red elastic, her hair was coarse and matted. Near the edge of the mask, where it traced the side of her face and along her jawline, was a garden of scabs and rashes. Raw red lines showed where the wooden edge had gouged flesh.

I rose from my desk. My steps boomed over the tile like distant thunder in the silent room. On the blackboard, Mrs. Lagrange had scrawled a line of symbols under the words *PYTHAGOREAN IDENTITY*. My back to the board, I looked down at the fallen queen.

Her motions stilled. The mask tilted up from the floor.

Behind the white eyes, through the dark holes, I saw nothing. I offered my hand.

Amelia's fingers were like twigs, wrapped in paper. As I helped her stand, I gripped her forearm and a hiss of pain reverberated behind the no-mouth. Releasing my grip, I saw bruises bloom where my hand had been. Her flesh had become delicate, vulnerable as a dream.

She stood before me.

I looked again into the holes of the mask's eyes. In the dark, narrow space where Amelia lived, her true eyes burned like newborn stars. No weakness in that burning, no fear. Pain, yes, and anger, and hatred deeper than any ocean. But not a glimmer of fear.

The mask turned away. Amelia stumbled picking up her backpack, and almost fell again, steadying herself on her desk.

I reached for her on instinct, but drew back, thinking of the bruises I'd already inflicted.

"Can you make it?" I said. "Are you all right?"

Her breath rasped against the wood. It was chilly, almost December, but she wore no jacket—I suppose by that point she didn't feel heat or cold. She fished in a pocket of her backpack, took out a notecard and ballpoint pen. Again, she scrawled a note, folded it, handed it to me.

As she left the classroom, walking slowly between the desks with their silent, unseeing students like a goddess among her idols, I unfolded the card. *ISAIAH 49:26*.

At lunch, none of the others would talk to me. I don't know what rumors they'd heard, what strange and awful versions of what had happened in Mrs. Lagrange's precalculus class. When I asked Thomas for his Bible, he passed it to me without a word.

Book of Isaiah, chapter 49, verse 26: *And I will feed them that oppress thee with their own flesh; and they shall be drunken with their own blood, as with sweet wine.*

———— ◦ ————

After school, I found the Strutts' address in the church directory. Biking to their house, I dismounted in the driveway and gazed up at the second floor. Behind the window, two white circles, a delicate nose, a smooth expanse. Behind the mask, a face I wished I could see.

The doorbell played a tinny hymn. From inside, I heard shouts, a body blundering against furniture. When Rev. Strutt opened the door, his shirt was half-tucked and his hair uncombed. He swayed in the doorway, his breath gin-sour, his eyes burning like embers.

"The fuck do you want?" he said.

"I'd like to talk to Amelia," I said.

He laughed, coughed, laughed again. "Be my guest," he said, stepping back and sweeping his arm in a mockery of welcome.

When I hesitated, he beckoned, snarling. "Are you going to fucking come in or not?"

I stepped across the threshold. The house smelled like sweat, trash, rot, the decayed wreckage of a home. From the entrance hall, I could see a living room full of overturned furniture, empty liquor bottles, and dirty plates teetering precariously on every surface. Finally my eyes landed on a stairway leading to the darkened second floor.

"About time someone came to see that girl," Rev. Strutt muttered, closing the door. "Fine bunch of people you are. Fine group of friends. No one for months. Orphan girl, all alone."

I looked away from him, embarrassed. I wasn't sure what I'd expected, but it hadn't been this.

"Well, she's not totally alone," I said. "She's got you."

"Ha!" He slapped his hand against the wall, hard. If it hurt, he was too drunk to feel it. "Me! And who comes to see *me*? No one. Widowed husband. Grieving. Lost my world, lost everything. These fucking people come to hear me read them the fucking Bible on Sundays; won't come help *me*! Leaving me alone with that girl, that—" He slapped the wall again.

Enough of this shit, I thought. I turned toward the stairway. "Amelia?" I called. "Are you up there?"

"She's up there, all right," Rev. Strutt said. "Always. I stay down here, she stays up there. Does she come down, help her poor father? Clean up a little, help around the house? No, nothing!"

"Listen, I'm not here for this. I'm here for Amelia. Did you ever think about the help she needs? When's the last time she ate?"

"She doesn't." He strode past me, and I followed him up the stairs. "Ever since she put on that goddamn mask. Too good to help her father. And now you're here for her. Who's coming to help me?"

The hallway upstairs was dark. I flipped the lightswitch, but no lights came on. Rev. Strutt hammered on a door, screaming in the dark.

"Amelia! You open this fucking door right fucking now!"

The weak light of late November spilled into the hallway as she opened the door. Amelia stood silhouetted in the feeble glow, her emaciated body seeming to float in the heavy, stuffy air of the house.

"About fucking time," Rev. Strutt said.

Amelia lifted a hand to the mask, pressed her fingers to the empty space beneath the delicate nose. Then, quick as a wish, she thrust her hand into her father's face. The twigs of her fingers scratched at his lips, pried his mouth open, squirmed into the darkness behind his incredulous snarl. The hallway echoed with a muffled shout, then a gargling yelp as a cord of muscle leapt on Amelia's arm, her arm thin and wasted but strong, strong. She pulled her hand back with a sodden rip. From her clenched fingers dangled a dripping rag of flesh, a puny, conquered banner.

In the dimness, the liquid pouring from Rev. Strutt's lips looked black as ink. He fell to his knees, clapped his hands over his mouth, bowed his head. Kneeling in the dark hallway, humbled before the mask, he seemed like a figure out of legend, a courteous knight paying obeisance to his lady.

The mask swung toward me. Just enough light fell through the doorway to show the birch-bark circles. The fiery points that shone from behind them needed no sun. The sparkle of sovereignty, bought at the price of absolute alienation. With gleaming eyes, Amelia gazed at me from a distance beyond endurance, a solitude past understanding.

I took a step toward her, quivering with terror and amazement. When her gaze didn't obliterate me, I took another. Soon I was at the doorway. Beside me, Rev. Strutt knelt in a pool of blood, his tongueless moans growing weaker.

He'd received the due punishment for his discourtesy. I strove to deserve better.

I raised my hands, pressing my fingers lightly to the sides of the mask. The wood was smooth and cool.

"May I?" I asked.

Ever so slightly, Amelia inclined her head.

As I lifted the mouthless veil, the squelch and stench of purulent flesh turned the hallway to a bower of corpse flowers, but I maintained my composure. I would be a courteous servant.

Freed from the smooth curve of the mask, Amelia's barbed maw glistened hungrily in the dying light. But I didn't flinch. I would be a courteous servant.

Her eyes blazed brighter, twin furnaces of devouring splendor. I returned their gaze, unblinking. I would be a courteous servant.

The shining eyes flickered down to Amelia's collapsed father, back up to me. Understanding, I nodded, found my way through the dark hallway and to the stairs. From behind, I heard the rustling squish as Amelia knelt on the blood-soaked carpet, heard the viscid rending of flesh torn from bone, the chewing and swallowing, the moans of satisfaction after long hunger. I heard it all, but I kept silent, and I never turned to look. It's impolite to watch your queen eat.

An Inherited Taste

Nadine Aurora Tabing

When Felisia was born, Bea wept with relief. The weight of her family's sorrow had been growing for some time, without anyone to carry it but herself. So, with care, Bea started on her daughter early.

She salted Felisia's milk and formula with murmured complaints. She pureed bananas and seasoned them with sparkling shreds of spite. She stewed potatoes and peas with stubborn little grudges, acidic—which also helped them keep well in their containers, and made only subtle hisses when she unscrewed the jar lids to ladle their contents into plastic blue spoons.

It was how Bea was raised herself—just a touch of rancor at a time. She'd squirmed through years of spoonfuls droning down her throat, too, and was rewarded with a palate so fortified she could bear even the most bitter grievances with an easy laugh.

Her husband, not so carefully weaned, couldn't stomach even the smallest disappointments: a bypassed promotion, a coworker who laughed too loudly, the engine light flickering in the car, a stubbed toe, his steak overdone on one end. His troubles made him slow, heavy, tired. On their first date, that first time he grumbled to her across the table about some old ex, she opened her mouth to take a brief, deep breath. The lingering boil of his disillusionment laid a grease on her tongue, which she swallowed alongside a mouthful of wine, hiding any residue behind a smile. He blinked. He straightened, and rubbed his shoulders with obvious awe at their sudden lightness.

You see? her mother had said when Bea told her he scheduled a second date. *You're all set now, anak, for a cheaper price than school, and look—not even your father was able to give me this.*

A white house. A white fence. A large white car whose creamy leather seats purred and heated. Even with all that, her husband needed her more, just as Bea's mother had hoped for her. Traffic, slow internet, delayed work projects, taxes, bills—he couldn't get through it all alone.

Every day the complaints were different, but they always tasted the same. Bea took them all, gnashed them to a paste while she cooed. Over the years, she became acclimated to it—her throat hardly burned anymore, her stomach hardly ached. She felt only the brush of rattling heat against her teeth, which she made herself bear with a calm smile.

Then, one day, they stopped serving ramen in his office cafeteria. And his bonus didn't come. And an outside agency was given ownership of his project. And a client side-eyed his tie, which he later found grease on, grease that Bea should have seen and cleaned for him, because what else was she doing all day? Didn't she care that he could lose his job because of this? His whole *career*?

Felisia was watching, with wide eyes from behind Bea's legs. She'd grown tall enough now that her little fingers could curl into the back of Bea's knees.

"Your tie? Oh no, I'm so sorry I missed that! Here. I'll fix it for you." Bea held out her hand. He yanked the tie from around his neck, balled it up, and threw it at her, missing her hand completely. Felisia dashed to pick it up, but before she could, Bea snatched it, and Felisia, into her arms. Then she walked upstairs, slowly, calmly, as her husband's voice swelled and rattled the walls.

"Shhh," she murmured, but it wasn't necessary. Felisia's eyes were dry, her expression pensive, as if puzzling over something new. She'd already learned to swallow her own tears, before her father could hear them and come storming in to silence her with petulant roars about the peace he needed after a long work day.

In the laundry room, Bea swabbed and scrubbed the tie with a thumbprint of pale detergent, then took her time looping it over a hanger to dry, taking as long as she could. Once some time of quiet passed, she led Felisia back downstairs, where she poured a small cup of chocolate milk that Felisia drank without even a flicker of distress at the flung bowls and spilled stew that littered the kitchen.

Bea felt a stirring in her. Something new. A strange little sharpness of hope.

"You are so strong," she told Felisia, clutching her close once the mopping was done. "Stronger than him. Stronger even than me."

More than that, Felisia was hungry. She crunched carrots and apple slices as she sat on the counter, legs swinging. As Bea cooked, she spared Felisia the best bites of breakfast and lunch and dinner.

Bea had suffocated her own aspirations for the privilege of this beautiful white house, old hopes for her future that were too big to support alongside her husband's abundance of calamities. She told Felisia about each one, her own choicest morsels. A degree in Landscape Architecture, a side gig singing, even one saccharine daydream of opening a shop to sell only made-from-scratch macarons—all were pried out stinging, and Felisia was eager to hear each one, her hands reaching.

"Tell me more," she said, and Bea, indulgent, continued. She told her of the recipes she'd inherited and kept hidden away, because her husband hated the smell of vinegar and fish sauce.

"Tell me more," Felisia said, and Bea, hesitant, continued. She told her of the friends she'd lost and was forbidden to see again, each name a rancid tang: Gianne who'd said *A white house isn't worth this*, Skyler who'd asked *And, eating someone's else's sorrows—that's all you think you're good for?*

"Tell me more," Felisia said, "tell me *more*." And Bea tried, she tried. There was so much more yet: the mornings she woke alone, the years of sidelong thoughts she had not been able to share with anyone, the fact that she had always wanted a house that was green. But Bea could not release any of these. She only coughed, struggling for breath around the knot in her throat.

That was the problem with swallowing sorrows—when they were lodged too deep, it was hard to push them out again. Eyes watering, Bea gazed at Felisia, and found she could not disgorge her deepest and first sadness, forced between her teeth and planted in the pit of her stomach soon after she was born.

My mother said this was how it always was for her, and so how it always would be for me. She said this is what's needed, to survive a world ruled by unhappy men. And I always accepted it.

But now came a newer sorrow.

I don't want this fate to be yours.

It was slick and sour. The sharpest sadness she'd ever tasted. Even after years of experience, Bea couldn't make it go down: it kept heaving up, so when her husband came home, fuming about lazy staff members, she could only barely manage to say, "That's awful, you don't deserve that, no one deserves that." She couldn't make it sound the way it needed to.

His eyes fixed on her immediately.

"You don't mean that."

"I do," Bea said, and then, again, forcing her tongue through a thickness: "*I do.*"

Felisia watched, silent, chewing her thumb, absorbing—just as Bea had when she was young—hanging on to the tranquil lilt of her own mother's words, memorizing and tracing the way she bent backwards to every frustration.

She'd survived, and all it took was chewing through years of cleaning, cooking, laughing when no one thought she could understand the muttered gossip about her being nothing more than a mail-order bride, arriving all packaged up and shiny with all the necessary accoutrements: knowledge of how to cook red meat, how to inflate an ego, how to drain depression. She'd survived, in a space small and hard and cramped, no wider than the breadth of a smile.

Felisia would grow up smiling for different reasons. She had to. She *had* to. Bea would make sure of it.

The next morning, she packed their clothes—enough to cover a week on the run. She had no money to bring, but she'd had skill enough to figure out this life—she could figure out another one, couldn't she? For the first time she could remember, she felt a stab of something in her chest that was hot and hopeful. She was reckless. She pulled out of the driveway and stared at the sky, breathless with how vast it looked suddenly—how endless—and how light she felt, having abandoned in that white house her every anguish and resentment. How many years had she thought her dragging feet and short breath was simply what living felt like? How long had she nursed all of that in her, devouring her and her husband's misfortunes both, so that only he had the freedom to move like this?

But when they made it to the highway, Felisia began to whine, loudly, and only kept getting louder. She thrashed in the car seat. She clutched her belly. She screamed.

"Mama! I'm *hungry!*"

There was a rest stop not far ahead. Bea peeled into the parking lot and clawed through the luggage, murmuring urgently, unraveling plastic wrap, unscrewing a thermos. But Felisia would not be sated by sandwiches or crackers or petty worry, nor even by the stress that boiled up in Bea's chest when passersby began to stare. Felisia swatted away the spoon her mother leveled before her mouth, splattering sauce on the car's leather seats. She continued to sob, inconsolable, starving. She only calmed when Bea's hands lowered with pained resolution.

Bea turned the car back. She pulled into the white house's garage, dabbed the leather seats in desperation, unpacked her life back into its cage.

Felisia's tears dried.

"The car's parked too close to the door," her husband said when he came home. Even expecting his suspicion, having spent the past hour steeling herself for it, Bea cringed.

"It's not grocery day," he continued, low. "Where did you go?"

Nowhere, Bea wanted to say. But he would have checked the gas level.

She said, "We ran out of steak."

It was plausible. She was already in the process of tenderizing dinner, to hide her shaking hands.

She had never lied to him before—had never risked it. She buried and armored herself in his disquiet, learned the borders of his temper, retreated when necessary, and never trespassed far enough to give him reason to do more than raise his voice. But now—God, if he made a move toward Felisia—Bea was ready, she steeled herself, she could take this tenderizer and—

"Be sure to buy enough next time," he said finally. "It's a waste of gas, and I don't want to have to keep remembering things for you. I have enough to worry about. God, the *day* I had ..."

He kept going. No shouts? No demands? He was letting her off the hook? Awed, she could hardly listen, and so when he paused and waited for her to dole out her usual comforts, Bea fumbled.

"I'm so sorry, Papa," Felisia volunteered. "That's awful."

Both parents looked at her, as if seeing her for the first time.

"That's right," he said. "It is awful. You get it, Felisia," and before Bea could think of some strategy to stop him, he went on: "You know what else? I'm positive one of those assholes filed a complaint against me."

"Oh no," Felisia said, nearing him, eyes wide.

"'Oh no' is right! It's the third complaint on my record now. What do you think that'll look like on my performance review?"

Felisia licked her lips. "... bad?"

"That's right. *Bad*. Fucking terrible. Hideous. I could lose my job. I could lose my whole *career*. And then where will you be, huh? You and your mom, useless here at home, not knowing anything about how to survive in this world."

He went on—he didn't hold back, not even to a child—but Felisia was nodding, and leaning, and reaching out, and then her father took her into his arms, jogging her, pacing, and all the while ranting and ranting and ranting. As Bea watched, Felisia wrapped her arms around his neck, and rested her head against him, eyes shut.

Relishing.

Bea felt her husband's misery radiate against her lips—that heat, that bite. As she had countless times before, she opened her mouth, and felt his fury coil into the pit of her stomach. Pungent. Salted. Like fermented vegetables. Cabbage or radish or something with crunch, so fresh that when she laid a hand on her belly she could almost feel it squirm. She didn't fight, as she always had. Took a breath. Let herself relax. Let herself digest.

For just a moment.

"Fucking exhausting," her husband was saying. "I'm sick of this. I'm sick of feeling this way. God, why am I the only one that ever feels this way? You never fucking lift a finger to help me. My life is a wreck. I can't handle this. I can't."

For the first time, she saw that perhaps he really couldn't. He was slumping with the weight of it. More sorrows than any one person could possibly bear.

"It must be so hard," Bea said. "That you're going to be trapped forever in some miserable company. If not that one, then the next. That no matter how hard you work, you'll hardly have enough to retire."

He looked up at her, agape, eyes dark. "W-what? What are you saying?"

"That's what I hear all the time. On the news, while I'm cooking. A recession coming. All the layoffs. And everyone saying it's just a way for these awful companies to make you scared enough not just to stay, but give everything for their deadlines."

He stared at her. Felisia clutched him as his arms slackened, slightly. Bea took Felisia from him, kissed him, held his hand, guided him to the dining table, gave him his steak, his wine.

"But don't think about that too much. There's nothing you can do about it. And don't let it go to your head! They're saying stress is the new smoking, it's just as dangerous, that it'll get you sooner than anything else, nowadays."

His first glass went fast. Bea poured him another, which Felisia helpfully pushed closer to him, until his fist unclenched to take it.

"I can't handle this," he said, toward the distance. "I can't."

Bea dragged up a chair beside him. Gently, she set Felisia down on his lap, where she leaned against him and set her ear against his beating heart, inhaling, chewing delicately, savoring. Together, they smiled as Bea patted his back, as she murmured into his ear.

"Go on, darling. Tell us more."

Anger Management

J. Rohr

Morning began with Mrs. Dobbs feeding the meat bag that Mr. Dobbs recently procured. She liked the looks of this one. Mrs. Dobbs suspected it wouldn't expire as quickly as the last.

In the basement, she spooned oatmeal for the chained-up sturdy sack. Though it asked stupid question after stupid question, she smiled rather than respond harshly. A part of her felt pity for something so foolish. After all, the thing should know she couldn't say much to it. That might imply it was human, and despite any speck of truth, as Professor Münsterberg's books insisted, to imply as much would be cruel.

Still, she fed the bag breakfast. It ate reluctantly, then ravenously, and Mrs. Dobbs took that as a compliment. Earlier she added a drizzle of maple syrup along with a sprinkle of brown sugar to sweeten the steel-cut oats. Even for a meat sack, breakfast is the most important meal of the day. No reason it shouldn't be a delight.

Humming softly, she took the dirty bowl back upstairs. The cries of the bag were muffled the second Mrs. Dobbs closed the basement door. Mr. Dobbs sat at the table reading the morning paper. He smiled at the sight of his wife. She returned the expression warmly.

"Good morning, dear," she said on her way to the sink.

"Morning," Mr. Dobbs said. Shaking the paper, he wagged his head sadly saying, "The world is a shambles lately."

"Hard to believe on such a sunny day," Mrs. Dobbs said.

Rinsing the bowl, she looked out the kitchen window. The view confirmed her notion. The world was full of bright sunshine.

They heard a faint banging. No doubt the sound of the chained-up bag trying to break free. It happened so often the Dobbses knew the sound all too well. Mr. Dobbs kept promising to install better restraints, something that wouldn't allow the meat sacks to pound on the pipes. The latest racket from below only fueled her increasing impatience for improved shackles, although Mrs. Dobbs also accepted this one was fresh. It had yet to learn the futility of its situation.

"What time is it?" Mr. Dobbs asked.

Glancing at a wall clock, Mrs. Dobbs informed him.

"Ah shucks," Mr. Dobbs said with a heavy sigh. "It's always too early or too late."

"How's that, dear?" Mrs. Dobbs asked.

"Just seems like there's never enough time," he replied.

Getting a cup of coffee, she sat at the kitchen table. Her husband folded the newspaper. He opened his mouth to say something, seemed to think better of it, then shook his head.

"I know the feeling," Mrs. Dobbs said. "Which reminds me. Sugar pie! Hurry up. Breakfast is getting cold."

They heard the rapid patter of footsteps on the second floor. The *thumpi-ty-buh-buh-bump* of their daughter racing around. Mrs. Dobbs smirked. Daughter Dobbs inherited her father's tendency to move at the last minute, a trait Mrs. Dobbs used to find annoying until she worked it out hammering a meat bag's bones soft.

However, instead of racing to the kitchen, Daughter Dobbs paused halfway down. She strode into the kitchen slowly, almost hesitantly.

"Mornin', sleepy head," Mr. Dobbs said.

"Hi, uh," Daughter Dobbs stood in the doorway chewing her lower lip. "I know I gotta get to school, but I was wondering about something."

"What's on your mind, kiddo?" Mrs. Dobbs asked.

"Which of you has been reading my diary?"

Mrs. Dobbs knitted her eyebrows together. She looked at Mr. Dobbs, who sat with his face tight.

"I know one of you has," Daughter Dobbs said. "So please don't deny it."

Mr. Dobbs stood up.

"I did," he said.

"Oh, Greg," Mrs. Dobbs said. "That's just not right."

Mr. Dobbs nodded. He fell back in his chair. He looked towards his wife though not in her eye.

"She came home crying the other day," he said. "And she wouldn't say why. I didn't know what to do and I was worried. Our daughter comes home from a date crying—I just thought the worst. I needed to know."

Daughter Dobbs sighed. Her shoulders relaxed. Taking a seat at the kitchen table, she took hold of her father's hand. Her eyes sparkled with fire.

"I appreciate you being honest," she said. "But I'm still hurt."

Sighing heavily, Mr. Dobbs patted his daughter's hand.

"I know," he said. "Look, sweetheart, even if it makes you late for school, why don't you take some time in the basement?"

"Really?" she beamed.

"Yeah," Mr. Dobbs said. "I got a fresh meat bag last night. Go to town."

"Remember," Mrs. Dobbs said, then quoted Professor Münsterberg. "*You need to get it out of your system before it grows toxic.*"

Daughter Dobbs jumped up. She kissed her father on the cheek.

"Thank you, Daddy!"

She raced off to the basement, snapping the door shut behind her. Mrs. Dobbs smiled. Whatever her daughter felt, she wouldn't take it out on family or friends.

Downstairs, the meat sack heard soft footsteps in the dark. Light streamed in through narrow windows, cracking the darkness. Not enough to tear away the shadowy veil. The meat sack could only just barely discern a silhouette slinking towards it.

A girlish giggle sounded.

"Who's there?" the sack asked in a trembling voice.

A soft ping preceded a noise like the scrape of something metal dragging across concrete. The punching bag made out the silhouette of a young lady in a poodle skirt before she sprang forward, swinging an aluminum bat.

"You asshole!" Daughter Dobbs shouted.

Every swing worked the body like a star hitter going for a homerun.

"That's my diary, you prick!"

"Help!" the meat bag hollered. "Help me!"

"Mind your own goddamn business," Daughter Dobbs snarled.

"Stop it!"

Daughter Dobbs pummeled the thing.

"Leave." *Wump!* "My." *Thud!* "Things." *Crack!* "Alone."

She tossed the bat aside, sent it clattering across the concrete floor. The meat sack sagged, yet its restraints kept it upright. Every inhalation ached horribly, and the punching bag groaned in sweaty agony.

"That's what you get."

The young lady's face shifted swiftly from a gargoyle expression to one sweeter than shoofly pie. She skipped off, disappearing into the shadows. The punching bag heard rapid footsteps on stairs, then light spilled down before being cut off by a closing door.

Before it shut, the young lady sang out merrily, "All better!"

———◇———

Mrs. Dobbs strolled through the house sorting the mail. Bills went on the secretary desk in the study. Junk mail went in the trash. The postcard went on the fridge. Affixing it with a magnet, Mrs. Dobbs smiled.

On the front was a Rockwellian family laughing at the beach. On the back, an ink-stamped symbol. A series of arrows coiled around one another—not unlike a Celtic knot—before each went off in its own direction. The tangle implied linear, direct courses that lost their direction due to some indirect influence, creating unnavigable knots. That's the explanation Mrs. Dobbs read in Prof. Münsterberg's first book. The symbol also denoted communication between practitioners of his Gestalt-inspired methodology. It was meant to encourage believers to stay true to Prof. Münsterberg's ideals, the practices his books encouraged.

Mr. Dobbs, home from work, was pacing and muttering angrily to himself.

"Hello, dear," Mrs. Dobbs said. "Is something the matter?"

"One more year," he snarled. "They said one more year then Greg *old buddy*, 1985 is gonna be your year. Promotions, pay raise—and I swallowed all their whole fucking bullshit."

"Language," Mrs. Dobbs frowned.

Her husband opened his mouth, clamped it shut again, and ground his teeth. Nodding more and more vigorously, he held up a finger. Then he stormed off, into the basement.

"That's better," Mrs. Dobbs said. "Like the good Professor says, *There's no reason to be rude to the ones we love when it's others who've hurt us.*"

She smiled. It was good to know her husband would work his feelings out on the meat bag rather than inflicting them on the family. Knowing he'd be thirsty afterward, she poured a tall pint of fresh, homemade lemonade. Leaving it on the kitchen table, Mrs. Dobbs went into the living room with a book. There she barely heard any sounds from the basement.

The fall evening appeared positively picturesque through the window. Her husband screamed in the basement, expelling the beast through bellows. Mrs. Dobbs smiled and waved to neighbors out for an evening stroll.

The front door opened and Daughter Dobbs stepped inside.

"Hey Mom," she called out. "Sorry I'm a little late. Band practice went long."

"That's okay," Mrs. Dobbs said. "I figured as much."

"Where's Dad?"

"Oh, honey, he went straight in the basement when he got home."

"Straight down?" Daughter Dobbs blanched, setting her book bag by the stairs. "Must've been a really bad day."

She chewed her lower lip, hesitant to go in the kitchen—anywhere near the basement door. Mrs. Dobbs understood her concern. Unfortunately, there were too many kids whose parents treated their own families like punching bags.

"There's fresh lemonade in the fridge," Mrs. Dobbs said. "Come on, I'll pour you a glass."

"I think I'll just be upstairs until Daddy's done."

"Don't be rude," Mrs. Dobbs' eyes sparkled. "I'm offering you a kindness."

The girl nodded. She followed her mother into the kitchen. Mrs. Dobbs prepared a fresh glass for her daughter. Daughter Dobbs thanked her.

Taking a sip, her eyes found the basement door. Mrs. Dobbs figured this would be a good chance for her daughter to learn to have faith in Professor Münsterberg's method. It was psychological science after all.

They heard heavy footsteps pounding up the stairs.

"I have homework," Daughter Dobbs said.

"It can wait," Mrs. Dobbs said with a mellow lilt. She set a hand on her daughter's shoulder. "Besides, we should be here to thank your father for not inflicting his bad emotions on us."

"What if he's still angry?"

"Nonsense," Mrs. Dobbs said, forcing a tight smile.

The basement door opened. Mr. Dobbs stepped out. Blood spatters covered his white-collar shirt. It looked positively polka dot.

"Hello, dear," Mrs. Dobbs said with sunshine in her voice. "Feeling better?"

"Much," Mr. Dobbs said, wiping sweat off his forehead with the back of his hand. "Goodness, would you look at me? I'm a mess. That monkey-wrench just drizzled all over the place."

Mr. Dobbs unbuttoned his shirt. Not wanting anything to drip on the carpet, he bundled the bloody clothes into a ball, then hurried into the garage to toss it in the wash before heading upstairs for a shower.

While he did that, Mrs. Dobbs sent Daughter Dobbs into the basement to fetch steaks out of the freezer. Those would thaw for tomorrow—a little weekend grilling always helped Mr. Dobbs relax. Dutiful daughter, the girl quickly did as she was told, pausing only a moment to eye the meat bag.

It hung limp on the chains. Blood drooled from the corner of its mouth. Teeth littered the floor. A dark purple mound sealed a swollen eye.

Satisfied her father had gotten it out of his system, Daughter Dobbs hurried back upstairs.

At her mother's request, she helped make dinner. The two sang along with the radio as they pan-fried chicken. When Mr. Dobbs returned downstairs, he found his family in the dining room chatting merrily.

"This smells delicious," he said, taking a seat across from his wife. "So, how was school?"

"It was alright, I guess," Daughter Dobbs squirmed.

"You guess or you know?" Mrs. Dobbs said.

"Let me out of here!" The voice came up out of the basement. Daughter Dobbs's eyes went wide in the realization she didn't shut the basement door. Jumping out of her seat, she rocketed to shut it. Closing the door in time to cut off another cry – "Someone hel..."

Sheepishly, Daughter Dobbs scurried back to her seat.

"Sorry," she said.

"It's okay," Mrs. Dobbs said. "You were telling us about school."

"You know, honey," Mr. Dobbs said. "When I was your age, if my dad asked how school was, I'd tell him 'nothing'— even when something happened. I guess it's just part of being a teenager."

"Even if it is a little rude," Mrs. Dobbs said, cutting into her lemon butter chicken.

"Alice Fletcher is having a party this weekend," Daughter Dobbs said quickly. "She invited me to go."

"Honey," Mr. Dobbs said. "Do we know the Fletchers? Or at least Alice?"

"Not that I know of."

Daughter Dobbs explained Alice Fletcher didn't usually hang out with people like her.

Mrs. Dobbs wondered what that meant. It turned out Daughter Dobbs didn't rank too high on the totem pole. The high school hierarchy often forgot she existed. However, allowing the sparkling zenith of teenage society—Alice Fletcher—to copy her chemistry notes earned Daughter Dobbs an invitation to the party.

"Well," Mrs. Dobbs said. "I'm surprised."

"What do you mean?" Daughter Dobbs asked.

"Who wouldn't want to hang out with you?"

A fresh round of muffled cries rose from the basement. Mrs. Dobbs frowned at another cacophony of clanging chains. Her eyes sparked with fire.

"What kind of party is this?" Mr. Dobbs asked. "I don't want you going to any keggers."

"It's not a kegger."

"Are her parents going to be there?" Mrs. Dobbs asked.

Both parents eyed their daughter. Avoiding their gaze, Daughter Dobbs shrugged as she pushed food around her plate. Mom and Dad glanced at one another. Mr. Dobbs raised an eyebrow.

The clanging downstairs ceased.

Mrs. Dobbs felt the tension leave her neck. Still, she was tempted to shoot her husband with a side eye. If he just got around to installing better restraints like the ones outlined in Professor Münsterberg's latest book, this wouldn't be an issue. Instead, they had to sit here with the sound souring the lovely dinner she'd prepared.

"Greg," Mrs. Dobbs said. "Please, stop teasing her. We're going to let you go after all."

"Really?!" Daughter Dobbs positively glowed.

"Yeah," Mr. Dobbs said. "Mother knows best."

"You're a good kid," Mrs. Dobbs said. "And we trust you."

"*Ohmygod*," Daughter Dobbs stood up. "May I be excused? I have to call Alice."

Her parents waved her away. Mr. Dobbs leaned back in his chair. He sighed.

The clanging started again. The muffled shouts soon followed.

———•○•———

When Mr. Dobbs opened the front door to the police, his knees buckled at the sight.

"Are you alright, sir?" the officer asked.

"He'll be okay," Mrs. Dobbs said coldly from behind her husband. "It's just a shock to see you here. Bringing our daughter home."

"I understand, ma'am."

The police gently pushed Daughter Dobbs into the house. They didn't step inside, staying instead on the doorstep, no doubt observed by circling gossip hounds. Mrs. Dobbs could already sense the dozens of eyes watching, their neighbors drawn to the flashing blue and red lights.

Mrs. Dobbs took a firm hold of her daughter's arm. She pointed the sobbing teenager towards the living room sofa. Daughter Dobbs knew to plant herself there without question.

The police filled in the details. Turned out Alice Fletcher's party was a kegger.

"If I may," one officer said. "Most polite kid I ever had to deal with. I don't think she's a bad seed."

"Thank you kindly," Mr. Dobbs said.

"Indeed," Mrs. Dobbs gritted her teeth.

The officer tipped his hat and Mr. Dobbs closed the door. Once the police drove away, Mrs. Dobbs glared at her daughter. Eyes smoldering like burning coals, she didn't have to say a word to burn her daughter.

She zipped across the room, straight for the meat bag.

"Well," Mr. Dobbs said—the basement door slammed shut. He flinched. "It seems you lied to us."

Blood curdling screams soon punched right through the floor. The usual muffling provided by the door failed. Banshee shrieks stabbed into ears, telling of the nightmare unfolding below.

As Daughter Dobbs and her father started arguing, their raised voices almost drowned out the horror show beneath them. The girl insisted she didn't lie. She didn't know there would be alcohol at the party. She swore she didn't have a drink. Her father sniffed the air, and though he didn't notice any boozy aromas, it hardly mattered.

"I wasn't drinking," she said. "How many times do I have to say it?"

"There was alcohol at the party," Mr. Dobbs said.

The cries in the basement died down but did not stop.

"So what?" Daughter Dobbs said.

"*So what?*" Mr. Dobbs folded his arms across his chest. "Where is this attitude coming from?"

"You say you trust me, but when I do the right thing you get pissed."

"Language." Mr. Dobbs started to pace. Shaking his head, he said, "You stayed at a party where kids were drinking. That's hardly *doing right*."

Silence.

Not just in the living room but also below. Mr. Dobbs and Daughter Dobbs stared apprehensively at one another. The basement door creaked open.

Motioning for the girl to stay put, Mr. Dobbs entered the kitchen. He found his wife standing beside the sink, filling a small glass with water. Her blue blouse was now crimson. Blood dripped from her hands. In the tense silence, each drop sounded like tiny hammers.

"Hey, honey," Mr. Dobbs said. "Feeling better?"

"Mmmhmm," Mrs. Dobbs nodded as she took a long drink.

Despite the mellow tone of her voice, Mr. Dobbs kept his distance. Meanwhile, Mrs. Dobbs looked out the kitchen window. Where some would see only darkest night, she saw a pleasant starry sky. It possessed the impression of famous art, and made her smile, a look the stains of blood smeared into something hideous.

Her husband staggered back at the sight of his wife. Red covered her face. Chunks of skin hung tangled in her hair. Absentmindedly, she picked bits of viscera from under her fingernails. She flicked them in the sink.

"I'm sorry, Mommy," Daughter Dobbs said.

Mr. Dobbs spun around, unaware his daughter had come into the kitchen behind him. He started to hustle her out, then froze as his wife spoke.

"It's okay, sugar pie," Mrs. Dobbs said in a honeyed voice. "I got it all out of my system. And I'm sorry, Greg. I know you probably needed a few minutes too, but I think I broke the bag."

"It's okay," Mr. Dobbs held up his hands. "These things happen."

"You're too kind," Mrs. Dobbs blew him a kiss. "I'm going to get cleaned up then see about getting us a replacement."

She started to exit. Her feet squished with every step. A trail of red footprints tracing back to the basement. He swallowed hard wondering what kind of mess was downstairs.

Before leaving the kitchen, Mrs. Dobbs paused to open her arms wide. She pulled her daughter into a tight, wet hug. Releasing her, she ventured upstairs.

Stained red, Daughter Dobbs just stood in silence. Her father placed a gentle hand on her shoulder.

"It's alright," he said. "She got it out of her system."

The Man Outside

Simone le Roux

When Imogen first saw the man outside, she didn't hesitate to tell her mom.

It was the strongest instinct her eleven-year-old brain had: If something was wrong, Mom would know what to do.

And something was quite wrong.

The man in the front yard stood motionless, watching the window Imogen sat on the other side of with such intensity that she found herself crouching behind the couch, as though his gaze would hurt her.

"There's a man outside, Mom," she squeaked and felt annoyed at herself. She was getting too old to run to Mom for every little thing that scared her.

Mom looked up from folding laundry at the dining room table. "A man?"

"He's watching our window."

Mom sighed, put down a freshly folded shirt, and stepped beside Imogen.

Imogen's hand itched to tug Mom down to her level, stop her from exposing so much of herself to this stranger's stare. But that would be silly. Mom pulled back the curtain for a better view and Imogen's hands clutched, white knuckled with the effort of stillness.

The first gentle hum of confusion in Mom's voice made Imogen curl into herself. Did Mom not see him? It *was* strange how he just stood, shrouded in shadow, eyes gleaming. It wasn't normal. Was Imogen imagining him? When Mom sent her out to play in the yard, would Imogen have to pretend that she couldn't see him either?

The reality was worse.

"Hmm ... oh, that man over there?" Mom pointed as though there were thousands of men standing just off the sidewalk to choose from. Imogen nodded anyway.

"I don't see the problem, dear," Mom said, dropping the edge of the curtain.

Breath left Imogen in a rush. "He's just ... watching," she choked out, dumbfounded.

"He's allowed to stand there, darling. He seems fine—he's just a man, like Dad or like your Grandpa," Mom added as the final blow.

For the first time in her short life, Imogen felt unsafe. Really, truly unprotected. The defensive part of her brain, the part meant to defend her from ugliness, whirred into gear, ready for damage control. Maybe Mom was right. After all, she would be better at spotting danger than Imogen, wouldn't she? Mom would know if this man was a threat, or if he really was like Dad or Grandpa.

"Should I go say hello?" Imogen asked, feeling as though it were Opposite Day. Down was up, danger was safe, and she had to do the exact thing she didn't want to do to calm the howling in her brain.

"Oh, *God* no," Mom said.

Imogen's heart twinged, because that wasn't the worried reaction that Mom had when she suggested taking the bus by herself or climbing the super tall tree in the park. Rather, Mom looked like Imogen had offered to lick the sidewalk or pee in public.

"What should I do, then?" Imogen whined, desperate to make things right, to reconcile the fear in her heart, to feel loved and protected and wanted by Mom again.

"What makes you think you have to do anything?" Mom said and threw another look at the man through the curtains. Their eyes must have met for a moment because she turned away quickly. "He's allowed to be where he is. There's nothing to be done. Period."

Mom heaved a sigh and returned to folding laundry. Imogen sank into the couch and cupped her hands over her chest, as though she could contain the explosion in her heart.

———•◦•———

The man was still there the next morning. He had not moved an inch.

Imogen knew because the snow all around his feet was pristine—she saw when she had to walk past him, as her legs endeavoured to go ever faster. His eyes were on her all the way down the street, an oily feeling down the back of her neck.

He was still there in the afternoon when Mom walked her home. Mom shot the man a quick, nervous smile like the one she gave the rude clerk at the post office, and ushered Imogen inside.

Imogen watched out the window for Dad to get home. While she didn't always see eye to eye with her father, she was certain he would see the same thing she did. He would tell the man to leave in his scary-calm voice and call the police, probably to let them know there was a strange man standing in gardens watching little girls. Not that Imogen was so little anymore.

She held her breath when Dad's car pulled up out front.

He stepped out, backpack slung over one shoulder, blinking in the cold winter air, and noticed the man immediately. How could he not? Imogen was sure he could sense the menace emanating from the man before he'd even stepped out of the car.

Dad's expression dropped into one of utter weariness, as though he had worked a million days in a row, only to find more work ahead of him. He pressed his lips together, nodded to the man, and walked inside.

After Mom's betrayal, Imogen couldn't bear it. She couldn't understand the despair rising in her chest like a wail, or why she knew she would never feel safe ever again. Perhaps, many years from now she would understand she was mourning—but in that moment, she felt only an emptiness so vast that it would echo like a cave if she fed any voice to it.

———————•◦•———————

The man did not shiver, did not sit down in the drifts of snow that surrounded his ankles. He stood and breathed and watched.

———————•◦•———————

Winter broke and gave way to warmer weather. Imogen kept her heavy jacket on well into spring, finding comfort in its cushiony layers. When Mom successfully hid it one morning, Imogen was forced to wear something more appropriate for the heat, and her skin crawled so badly that she had to clench her fists to stop herself from scratching at her bare arms.

She stopped playing in the front yard. She used to sit out on the swing with a pile of books next to her, feet kicking idly while she read. Now, she couldn't even relax enough to read in her own room unless she closed the curtains. Whenever she opened them, her eyes would find the man's already on her, always steady. She shuddered.

Over time, though, Imogen became used to all the ways she made herself feel safe: her carefully controlled eyeline, her permanently shut curtains that bathed her room in glowy gloom, the reassuring feel of her backpack. It was heavy enough to swing at the man if he finally attacked her. She had loaded it up with water bottles and stones.

And then, on one of the last days of the school year, as Imogen passed through the front yard, the man took a step forward.

At first, she was sure it was a trick of the light. But when she really looked, she knew. He had taken one big stride towards her house. He stood still again, gazing back at her as though nothing had happened.

Imogen threw up when she got to school, not knowing how to tell anyone. What would she say? What could she say? Her parents had only ever made excuses and she had no reason to believe her teachers would do any different.

"Are you okay?" a timid voice asked through the stall.

Imogen dry-heaved again before she was able to pause and consider. "I'm okay," she lied after a while. How could she sum up months and months of exhaustion? The terror of seeing that imposing figure move even closer to her home? Knowing there was no point in telling anyone because they would tell her not to worry when it was the only thing she could think about? "I'm just tired."

"I get that," the voice, another girl, said. "Sometimes I feel like there isn't enough sleep in the world."

<hr />

Months went by. Imogen's birthday came. Twelve years old: her whole life ahead of her, but not her front yard. Not if she wanted to feel safe.

One night, Imogen was fresh off a sugar rush and clutching her abdomen as though she could squeeze this new pain from it like toothpaste out of a tube. She dared to peek out of her curtain at the man and look. Really *look*.

He wasn't so scary, she thought. He was all broad shoulders and hands—like Dad's, like Grandpa's. Perhaps his aura of menace was something else. Intensity? Persistence? Determination?

Why would anyone spend all this time, all this energy on her, she wondered. She looked down at her little belly, her doe-like limbs. Perhaps he had noticed the way her hair caught the sun, or he had seen that she was particular about wearing clothes that flattered her new waist, like Mom taught her.

More and more, Imogen wondered what the man thought when he looked at her. Did he notice her shoulders slumped on bad days, her cheeks glowing on good ones?

He continued his excruciatingly slow journey across her lawn. Was he marking the time by the seasons that fell from his shoulders like nothing, or by Imogen's changing body?

"That figure's not going to last forever, hon," Mom would say and, God, Imogen hoped her mother was right. She couldn't bear the man's eyes on her, but she also couldn't imagine what she would do if he turned away now.

———◆◇◆———

The first time she noticed a different man standing in a different yard, she froze.

This man, too, stood with a straight back and hands that vibrated like they would blur into motion any second. He was a bit smaller than hers, a bit older, but there was no mistaking the shadows wreathing him, the way he watched the house.

No one else she knew had someone in their front yard, but this person did—and it took everything in Imogen not to run up to their front door and knock. All she wanted was to talk to someone, anyone, who could understand how she felt.

But what if they didn't? What if they gave her the same cold, disgusted looks her parents did when she asked? What if they also found her fear just as shame-worthy as her curiosity?

She shoved her hands deep into her pockets and carried on home, like she would whenever she saw a man in a place where he had no business being.

———◆◇◆———

Imogen was sixteen. Earlier in the day, she'd seen the man take one of his big steps forward, placing him more than halfway across the lawn. She chewed at her lip so hard that it bled.

How dare he treat her like this without making his intentions known? How could he turn her own family against her with his mere presence?

Imogen was furious, but she didn't know who to direct it at. Herself, maybe, for being such a coward. Her parents, for telling her that her feelings were wrong. Her friends for not feeling the same way, for not having a man of their own inching ever closer to them. Her rage was all-consuming, directed at everyone and no one at all.

She waited until her parents were out to sneak some vodka from their liquor cabinet. She sipped from the bottle and glared at the man outside. A few gulps were enough to get her stumbling drunk, shedding her self-control.

Before she could counsel herself against it, she was storming outside in her pyjamas. Years and years of tacit warnings from her parents faded into so much background noise and she squared up right in front of him, fists clenched so hard that her nails dug into her palms.

"What do you want with me?" Imogen blurted. She didn't care about his glare or the way that he was much taller than she'd thought he would be this close. Their eyes met for an instant and his hatred matched her own.

He didn't reply, just kept his eyes boring into hers. His hands twitched.

"Imogen, what do you think you're doing?"

Mom and Dad were back early. Date night hadn't gone well, then.

"Leave that man alone this instant!"

Suddenly, she was eleven years old again, waiting for her parents to make her feel safe, to make her feel sane. To reconcile the fear in her heart, to love and protect her again.

"Just tell me why!" she cried, and she wasn't sure who she was addressing. Her fists shook and, to her utter dismay, tears began to trickle down her face. "What do you *want*?" she sobbed, swiping at her nose.

The only answer was her mother's rough grip, dragging her inside.

———◆———

Imogen did the math.

The man would reach her front door exactly two weeks after her eighteenth birthday, and she was quite sure no one would stop him.

Was it such a bad thing? This man, who had devoted so much time, so much focus, such discomfort to her, would at last step into her home. Didn't he deserve a break? Somewhere to rest? Would he at least reveal what was so special about her?

As much as she thought about it, Imogen couldn't decide what she was more excited for: the answers to her questions or the end of this ridiculous, disappointing march through adolescence.

Even when she got home later with her parents' permission, she found herself skirting the man, as if somehow her impropriety would jolt him out of his stoicism. She was sick of being nervous, of not understanding why. Of avoiding eyes, pulling up her necklines, pulling down her hemlines. She wanted it done. She couldn't wait.

Her eighteenth birthday came and went. She celebrated it at the park with friends. As she stumbled home, belly full of cake and cheap, warm whiskey, she had to weave around the man.

He was on the porch now. Frankly, a bit of a nuisance. Obvious. Even her parents, who had ignored his presence for years, became visibly irritated every time they tried to leave the house. One time, Mom rolled her eyes at Imogen, as though it was her fault.

Her calculations had been a bit off. Two weeks and three days after her birthday, there was a knock at the door. One solid fist pounding three times.

Her entire body buzzing, Imogen rushed downstairs. Her parents were already there, opening it. The man stood, a smile cracked across his face. It was bizarre. It would have been charming on anyone who wasn't her tormentor.

"Imogen, your guest is here," Mom said, as though Imogen had invited him in.

"Have anything to say?" Dad asked.

Looking at this man, who had haunted her, watched her, scared her, judged her, Imogen didn't know where to begin. How could she? No one had told her what to do from here. All these years to prepare, and no one had prepared her.

She took a tentative step forward.

As soon as she came close, the man's enormous hand snapped out and closed around her neck. He lifted her up, up, up, until her feet scuffed at the floor.

"What are you doing, Imogen?" Mom shouted, pushing ineffectually at her arm. "What did you say to him to make him behave like this?"

Imogen choked, clawed at the hand that grasped her throat. Even if she could say something, she wouldn't know how to make anyone understand what she felt. It wasn't betrayal exactly—she'd always been suspicious of the man's intentions and aware of her parents' indifference—and it wasn't sadness either.

This felt correct. Perhaps she could have teased the man less or kept her weighted backpack on her or not gotten drunk those times or asked her family the right questions or confided in someone at school. But she knew. Deep, deep down, she knew it was only ever going to end this way.

Her hands tired, weakening. They caught on her chest, where her fingertips felt her heart flutter like a dying bird.

As the Silence Burns

Sara Tantlinger

The first time Aponi swallowed silence, it rattled deep inside her bones, clinking around her skeleton as it tried to escape. She closed her eyes and imagined the silence as sentient, adorned with tiny dragonfly wings that fluttered madly. In her mind, the creature burst from her body, shattering skin and muscle into a waterfall of blood and flesh. But it was free, beating its smeared, shimmering wings out into the sunlight for all to see and hear, if they listened closely enough.

She learned a lot about silence at the tender age of thirteen as she followed her mother down the dirt-trodden path between the main river and the village. A bucket of water balanced precariously against her hip. She could not carry water as delicately as her mother. The late summer sun scorched the world, and though Aponi was thankful for the light and life of Helios, agony spread across her skin from the fierce burn. Fairer than her mother, she possessed the same cardinal-red hair, as if Helios himself dyed it with a molten beam from the sun's core.

Hair worthy of a phoenix, her mother often said, but she rarely talked any more about the creatures.

Aponi kept her eyes downward, squinting away from the sky's brightness. Instead, she focused on her mother's sandaled feet and the dry dirt. Her tabby cat, Hunter, who had also taken the journey to the river with them, pawed at some butterflies on the side of the path, half-chasing them when they fluttered away. The butterflies danced in the air with striking, blue-toned wings. Inky black spots decorated the center. Aponi envied their wings, both delicate and strong, able to bring a kind of freedom she knew she would never have. If only she could command her spine to grow wings of its own. She'd never come back to this place of heat and sand.

Be thankful for what you have. She heard her father's dulcet voice in her head, how he poured on the sweetness for when it came to being *thankful,* but if anything went wrong, such sweetness hardened into unrepentant ire. Father never tolerated rudeness. He demanded his daughters be respectful and grateful, or his wrath would surely match the sun god's anger.

"What are you thinking about back there, Api? You haven't been this quiet since Gram made you eat beet pie."

Aponi picked up her pace to match her mother's stride. "Argh! Thanks for that memory. I was thinking of Elie and Dora."

"Hm." Her mother paused. The village came into sight, half covered in shadows from a drifting cloud.

"Have you heard from your sisters?"

"They sent some letters, but nothing too interesting," she replied, telling almost the truth. Elie was happily married and traveling with her husband to forgotten cities. Dora, the oldest of the three, had secretly left the husband their parents suited her with. She did not tell Aponi what exactly she was doing in the meantime, but she claimed to be content in her new life away from that toad of a man. Aponi was sworn to secrecy unless Dora came home to visit and told their parents the news, but she doubted Dora would ever return after what happened.

Aponi did not mind this type of silence, the secrecy of protection. It was the quiet bond of sisterhood, not the kind of silence that burned from the inside. She longed to pursue the same independence. Even at thirteen, she knew she'd never be content with confinement, just like the butterflies.

Their blue wings fluttered above her, escaping to the skies and away from Hunter's playful paws.

"Keep up, Api."

She trotted back up to her mother's side, not even realizing she'd slowed her pace again. They entered the sweet shade of the tall oaks lining the village entrance.

A stretching shadow bent around the corner and a figure startled them as a man exited the gate.

Her mother stopped and lowered the bucket so she could give a small bow. Aponi followed her actions even though she hated the village watchers, especially Ezio. His eyes never seemed to be looking the same direction. He was a thin, aging man with unkempt yellow hair and even yellower teeth, but Ezio's power over the Village of Hestia was not to be ignored. He made that clear when he helped exile Dora from the community. Aponi held nothing but disgust in her heart for this man and his entitled sons.

He walked closer and his left eye focused on her.

"My, my. Little Aponi, nearly grown." He tilted his head and regarded her mother, his right eye unable to look at either of them straight, like a loose marble rolling around inside his skull. "She is getting to be quite lovely, isn't she? Dare I say, the loveliest of all your girls."

Aponi watched her mother stiffen and clutch the wide bucket of water tighter.

"I thank you for your kind words, Watcher Ezio."

Aponi knew it must kill her mother to say those words. Like her father, Ezio did not tolerate rudeness. To stand up against him would bring unspeakable consequences.

The older man grinned and Aponi caught a whiff of his rank, onion breath. Usually her mother wasn't afraid of anything, but anytime she saw Ezio, her hands trembled. A slight movement, but Aponi prided herself on her observation skills. She had even wanted to be a village watcher when she was little, hearing tales of how they protected everyone from invaders. The watchers were once regarded as wise and valiant, keepers of the history that Helios scorched into the earth. Her father, however, said girls can't be watchers and never let her speak of it again.

Ezio directed a knobby finger at Aponi and tucked a loose strand of red hair behind her ear. The reek from inside his mouth sent sour heaves to her gut. She wondered if his eldest son had onion breath too … and if he had breathed his wretched air onto Dora's face when he touched her.

"Little strawberry," Ezio said. "Growing up so sweet, so ripe. And you know—" he bent lower, closer to her ear now. "The juices only get sweeter with time. But not too much time or they weaken and rot. Bruises form easily on something so delicate. You have to pluck when fruit is the most delicious, Aponi."

She didn't realize she was shaking until Ezio bid them goodbye and disappeared back into the village, his head high, the way only a man who has never experienced any shame could.

"Come on," her mother said, lips in a tight line and her voice brusque.

"Mama ..."

"Come, Aponi. Now." Her tone softened enough for Aponi to understand they needed to get back to the house. It was not safe to discuss such things in the open. She followed quickly, hands shaking as she held the water bucket. Hunter disappeared, and so had the blue butterflies.

⸺◆⸺

After the chores of the day were finished, her mother called to her to come outside.

"Come child, let us give thanks to the stars. Did you know Hestia sacrificed her own fire to give us life? Without her, we would have no stars to pray to, or to guide us."

Aponi settled on the cool, earthy ground next to her mother, listening to cicadas sing near the pond.

"Look now, see those two stars? And the line they make below? It's hard to see now, for she usually isn't in full view until late autumn."

"She?"

"Queen Cassiopeia. A magnificent constellation."

Aponi peered at the dark sky and tried to make out the shape between the twinkling stars so far away. She wished she could fly right up there and touch their light. "Was she a phoenix, Mama?"

"No, but our ancestors prayed to her. Cassiopeia contains a vast number of young stars; she holds them in her body like a nursery of novae. She is brightest in the fall and represents the possibility of birth, of something new, which is why the phoenixes prayed to her. She hides more stars beneath her dust and winds than we will ever see. If you are ever lost, my dear Api, if you are ever scared, pray to Cassiopeia. She will guide you as she guided the phoenixes for so long ..."

"Until the purge?"

Her mother sighed and wrapped an arm around Aponi's shoulders. "Yes."

"Are there no phoenixes left, Mama? Did none fly away?"

"I don't know. It's possible, but unlikely. The village watchers were very ... thorough in what they did."

Aponi knew little of the details. Adults never seemed to want to talk about it, and most of the records in the library skirted around the details, likely because the watchers commanded them to be cleansed. They had seized control over the phoenixes somehow, she knew. They'd found a way to hurt the women born with powers in their blood. Phoenixes were only ever women, and the watchers found their mating with human males to be unnatural. Watchers claimed hell would rain down fire onto the village if this did not stop. So, they stopped it.

"Things weren't always like this," her mother continued. "The watchers weren't always lecherous bastards."

Aponi shivered. "Tell me more about the phoenixes, Mama."

Her mother pressed her lips against Aponi's head in a soft kiss. "My inquisitive, Api. Phoenixes were of the highest calling and no one trifled with them until—well, you know the story. Before these watchers who dare call themselves holy men came and ruined all. Phoenixes were mystical, good and caring; strong women who bore great, colorful wings like peacock feathers. They could sail high in the sky, above the birds. Some say they could fly nearly to Helios himself and their wings would protect them. And when they died, they could rebirth themselves from the ash. They did not fear fire. They controlled it. When they were truly tired and done with life, when it was time to pass their power onto another, they chose not to die in fire, but to die a certain death, and not rebirth their souls from the ash."

Aponi remained silent, thinking of the blue butterfly wings and if they could be reborn, too. Freedom, especially the freedom of flight, was the deepest craving she had ever known.

"Do you want to know a secret, Aponi?"

"Of course!" She sat up and stared, eager.

Her mother reached into the pockets of her faded dress and removed an object. Something shiny dangled from a thin, black rope. Aponi peered closer and recognized the flaming sun symbol of the phoenixes.

Her mother placed it around Aponi's neck and tucked the pendant beneath the collar of her dress. "This belonged to your great-grandmother, the last phoenix I ever had the chance to know."

Overwhelmed, tears formed in Aponi's eyes as she gently touched the necklace. "Great Gram was one?"

Her mother nodded, and a mournful look took hold of those emerald irises. "She led them for many years. Her fierceness made history, and even though the watchers destroyed the books of the phoenix's impact upon this Earth, they can never destroy the truth." She placed a hand on Aponi's cheek and kissed her head before standing up.

"Are we phoenixes, Mama?"

She looked away and then back toward Cassiopeia. "I don't think so. If we are, then our magic is trapped inside. Sometimes it skips a generation or two." She winked at Aponi and disappeared back into the house.

———— ◦ ————

Two days before Aponi's seventeenth birthday, she walked along the dirt path between the great river and the village, Hunter by her side. He stopped now and then to paw at crickets or meow at birds. She recollected a time some years ago when she had been returning with water, her mother walking ahead and Hunter by her side, chasing those blue butterflies.

The pendant her mother gave her that night sat neatly tucked beneath her dress collar. She felt its comforting weight on her chest as she carried the heavy bucket. Her sisters had written her for her upcoming birthday, but they would not be traveling home.

As Aponi grew older, she understood more about what happened with Dora, more about the intentions of certain men within the lonely village. Ezio's son, Lander, wandered the town freely, as if what he'd done to her sister meant nothing. To him, it probably didn't, but to Dora, it was an invisible branding of unimaginable pain.

The old man Ezio was not aging well. Aponi felt no remorse for him.

She shook her thoughts away and kept a steady grip on the water bucket. Dreaming of sprouting butterfly wings, picking up her mother, and carrying them both away to join her sisters. Hunter stopped in front of her and his tail bristled out.

"What's wrong, silly cat?" She paused and glanced around, seeing only the dusty lining of the trees before the village gate.

Snap.

The cat shot away as something broke in the woods. Aponi spun around and caught a shadow in her peripheral vision.

The devil himself. Lander.

"Morning, Miss Aponi," he said, a sly smile forming on his lips. He was less yellow in the mouth and hair than his father, but the aura of slime stunk from him just the same.

Cold sweat formed on Aponi's spine and stuck there, trapped between skin and dress fabric.

"I said," Lander stepped closer, a strand of hay sticking out ridiculously from between his teeth. "Morning. It's awfully rude not to respond to a village watcher."

"Good morning," she said between gritted teeth. "And you're not a watcher, yet."

He laughed, cold and without humor. "Soon enough, little strawberry."

Aponi's blood froze. How did he know that horrid nickname? Another thing he stole, plucked right from Ezio's rotting lips.

The trees rustled again, this time from where the twig had snapped. A softer, younger version of Lander stepped out from the foliage.

"You know my brother? Theo's about your age."

He was a year or two younger than Aponi and very quiet. She had never spoken to the boy. He looked even younger than his years, sickly almost, and was definitely the runt of Ezio's spawn.

"Told you she's pretty," Lander said and elbowed his brother in the side. "Even cuter than Dora, huh?"

Theo said nothing until his brother elbowed him again, harder, in the ribs. He winced, but something about his face told Aponi he was used to this treatment. "Sure, Lander."

Another smirk split its way across Lander's face. He spit the strand of hay out. "Come walk with us, Miss Aponi. There's a nice secluded spot in the woods. Maybe your big sis told you about it."

Fury shot through Aponi with heated bursts, gathering in her chest beneath the sun pendant. "Get out of my way."

Lander stepped in front of her again. "Come on, sweet girl."

"No."

That word was as good as a death sentence when it came to messing with the watchers or their kin, but right now, Aponi didn't care.

Lander held up his hands, palms splayed toward her and stepped to the side. She secured her grip on the water bucket and marched forward, the scorching sun beating down on them all.

Then, hands on her waist, tugging her body back.

The more she moved, the more precious water she spilled.

"Get off me!"

He held tighter and his hands drifted up toward the pendant.

She spun around and heaved the bucket with all her might at his head. It clunked loudly against his skull as water splashed everywhere, soaking both Lander and the parched dirt beneath him.

A shallow cut swelled above his eyebrow and blood dripped down his furious face. He wiped it away in rage and launched himself at her.

"You whore," he seethed, dragging her back into the foliage with his hand around her throat.

"Lander, leave her alone," Theo said, his voice soft and drowned out by Aponi's own yells. She thrust her head back hard and collided with Lander's nose. He staggered around but grabbed her necklace, breaking the string. The pendant soared into the dry grass, but at least Aponi saw where it landed. She bent to retrieve it, only to be met with Lander's heavy hands pushing her down.

"There's someone coming," the younger brother said.

Aponi heard rustles in the grass but couldn't see what was happening. Lander swore and then stuffed a cloth into her mouth. An acrid taste of old sweat stung her tongue.

"Get up and come with me or I'll make what happened to your sister look like good fun compared to what happens to you."

He forced her up and kept a tight hold on her arms, leading her away from the path and through the woods. As he shoved her past Theo, deeper into the shadowed trees, her mother's voice called her name from the path where the empty water bucket remained.

—◦—

"Look what I got, Father," Lander said and tossed Aponi onto the floor of a shack she'd never seen before. It sat deep in the woods, far from the village. If Ezio's family owned property out here, they'd never told anyone. The dilapidated hut contained one room, and long stalks of grass sprouted up between the floorboards.

Ezio sat in a rocking chair, looking more haggard than ever. "The strawberry?" He grinned, and his breath filled up the tiny room. He leaned closer to her. "Do you remember, Aponi, about the fruit and the right time to pluck? Well, this is it."

Lander removed the cloth gag from Aponi's mouth.

"You disgusting bastard."

He laughed and rocked in the chair. A kerosene lamp and a jar of oil sat on the desk opposite him. "You know what I used to do in this place, little strawberry? I used to take the phoenixes and show them a thing or two before their execution. Those days were the sweetest, the ripest ..." he trailed off and grinned, lost in his own vile pleasure. The shack's door squeaked and Theo walked in.

"Where've you been, child?" the old man growled, waving his youngest son away. "Eh, doesn't matter. Anyway, little Aponi, the phoenix stayed dead, you see. They didn't come out of the ashes ever again, and that's not how it was meant to be. I thought maybe your sister was the next one, thought she'd be good for Lander here, but it wasn't Dora. Turns out it's you." Every rock of Ezio's chair sent creaks to echo around the room.

"Teach her a lesson, Lander. We'll make sure the last of the phoenixes carries on our bloodline."

Vomit roiled with acid waves in Aponi's gut. "I thought the watchers hated the phoenix."

Ezio leaned forward. Most of his teeth were missing. "We sure do, strawberry, but that was because they wouldn't mate with watchers. They hated us, and so they had to pay. Now we have the chance to start something new, something powerful. Go on then, Lander."

He grabbed her wrist and hauled her back toward the door.

"No. Here."

"You sick, fucking creep," Aponi said and tried to squirm out of Lander's grip. He held on to her tight and forced her to the ground. She noticed Theo's hand clutched around something.

"That's mine!" She kicked at Lander, desperate to move.

The door rattled, flung open. A wave of red hair shone in the light. Hair just like hers.

"What the—" Lander didn't have time to finish his thought. Aponi's mother had slashed a small knife across his flank, leaving a superficial but bleeding wound. Aponi jerked away and Theo handed her the pendant without a word. She tied it back around her neck.

"He showed me this place," her mother said and nodded toward Theo. "Said his brother took you."

Ezio hurled himself out of his chair and shoved Aponi's mother toward the other wall. A sickening crack echoed when her head collided with an uneven shelf. Glass shattered from the fallen kerosene jar, knocked loose in the scuffle.

"Mama?"

The woman blinked but otherwise stayed still, dazed and bleeding.

Aponi kicked at the old man. Lander seized her with one arm and held Theo with the other as Ezio picked up a glass shard.

He glanced at Aponi with his one straight eye and sliced the glass across her mother's throat.

Aponi didn't know if she stopped screaming as the blood flowed down and mixed with the oil. The pendant burned against her, melting into the skin of her chest. The scent of cooked flesh filled the air; even her tongue tasted the salt of charred meat.

Lander shoved his brother aside and went after Aponi again. His nails scratched her flesh, but her elbow landed a solid *crack* against his jaw.

Fire consumed her inside out, searing through her ribcage. She did not hold her screams back.

Aponi had learned how acidic silence could be, a metallic bile heavy on her tongue. She screamed in rage and scrambled to the kerosene lamp as Lander pressed himself hard against her, sending nausea to root deeply in her burning chest. Spilled oil slicked the upper half of her body, and she hoped it would be enough.

Enough to grant her freedom, at last.

The pendant continued to scald as she thrashed an arm toward the desk to knock the lamp down. Her hand collided with the desk's leg and the lamp toppled over. It did not break.

Theo tugged at his brother's ankles, trying to haul him off Aponi. She used the distraction to splash more oil on her dress. Slippery hands grabbed the lamp, then smashed it against the floor.

"No!"

She thought the yelp came from Ezio but wasn't sure. Her fingertips found the cool hand of her mother as the flames sparked into a conflagration up her body, consuming them into an embrace that seemed to be sent from Helios himself. From Hestia. From Cassiopeia and from the phoenixes.

The pendant and flames burst together, surrounding her in a peaceful oblivion of searing wander.

She felt herself die.

Then, she breathed. Ashes. Little gray and black flecks, some still smoldering. They filled everything.

In this after-death place, she found a reflection of herself. Her body. The wings were magnificent as they stretched from her spine in a kaleidoscope of gold, orange, yellow, and blue feathers. Each barb and piece of plumage connected to her every atom and breath. The pendant was gone. In its place though, glowed the symbol of the phoenix, seared in gold on her skin.

She flew from the darkness and realized she'd soared right into the stars, touching the cloud dust of Cassiopeia. She was not alone. Phoenixes flew with her on every side, bringing fire and strength.

The peace within Aponi was greater than anything she had ever known. She knew her mother had found peace after death, that her sisters were safe. She knew the boy, Theo, who hated Ezio and Lander as much as she did, had escaped the forest with Hunter padding behind. Neither would be harmed.

She descended from the stars then, her wings pointing toward Earth as she decided how lovely it might be to see the whole village burn.

Acid Skin

Marisca Pichette

W hen I was twelve, I signed a contract for acid skin. On the floor of my childhood bedroom I made a summoning circle out of patterned socks, scrunchies, dollar store deodorant, and a box of Always pads. I copied sigils from a library book onto the wood with sidewalk chalk leftover from the summer. I cut off a chunk of my hair with craft scissors and burned it in a Bath and Body Works candle. Vanilla Bean Noel mixed with keratin smoke, and my daimon appeared.

Xe was small, with thick limbs of luscious ruby. Xyr tails curled around my makeshift circle, three tips flicking in time with my heartbeats. Xyr many eyes, when they met mine, were bathroom-tile white.

"You may regret it." Xe sounded like me—not my voice in recordings or videos, but my voice in my head.

I should've been afraid. I should've looked at xem and seen a monster. But when I looked at xem, all I saw was a chance. I knew who the real monsters were, after all.

"You don't know what I'm going to ask," I said, my tongue a dry, flopping thing trapped between my teeth. I wasn't scared. Nervous, maybe. Of what I wanted—of not getting it. Of my parents downstairs in front of the TV, oblivious.

My daimon smiled, three rows of perfect reptilian teeth. Xe spoke again with my voice. "I never come unprepared. Do you think we appear by lottery? You've been mine since you were born. I've known your mind for as long as you have. I know what you want from me."

I swallowed. I hoped my parents didn't smell the smoke from the candle and my hair. I picked at my cuticles, blood gathering under my nails. When I looked at my daimon, xyr eyes blinked in pairs. I remembered my wish, coiled in the space between my lungs.

"Why would I regret it?"

I rearranged my legs from cross-legged to bent together beside me. Cuts from my first attempt at shaving caught the candlelight. I picked at these too, drawing more blood. The pain was good. It distracted me from the memories that drove me here.

Why would I regret it? I couldn't think of anything that I'd regret less. I couldn't think of anything else that would make it safe outside. Nothing would protect me better.

My daimon paced within the circle, clawed feet eerily silent, tails sweeping up and down in waves. If my parents heard anything downstairs, it would be me, not xem. "You're young. You may wish to be touched when you're older. But if I grant your request ... that will be impossible."

I'd thought about this. There weren't any bodies or faces I wanted to hold. None I wanted to let hold me.

I'd made my decision—on the train, on the walk home. "No."

"No?"

"I won't ever want that."

Xe stopped pacing. Xe sat down, tails wrapped around xyr feet. I could feel xem studying me, thinking I was too young to turn myself invincible.

But not too young to know my vulnerability, I thought. Not too young to understand what could happen if I do nothing.

After long seconds, white eyes blinking at me in clusters, my daimon nodded. "Very well. Say the words."

It was getting harder to swallow. I tried anyway, forcing saliva over my tongue and down my throat–slick, hot, hollow. Xe watched me, all gazes still now, focused. I repositioned myself again, wiping blood from my fingers onto my knees.

"I, Kahlia Louise Lane, ask for protective skin. I want it to rip anyone who touches it, scald them, poison their pores. I want to be lethal."

My daimon swept xyr foot across smudged chalk sigils. The symbols morphed into text I could read: a contract chalked across my bedroom floor, the end punctuated with a stray hair tie.

"Sign," xe said.

I fumbled for the chalk I'd left outside the circle. My muscles were floppy, misaligned on my bones. I shook out my arms, reading and rereading the words before I leaned forward, putting my hand inside the circle with my daimon.

Carefully, I signed my name, dotting the I's with two little hearts. I pulled my arm out of the circle, releasing the chalk. It left my palm dusty and blue.

Xe closed all xyr eyes at once. "It is done."

Xe disappeared, the candle snuffing into scented smoke. Sitting alone in my bedroom, I felt my clothes begin to melt around me.

———✦———

It's not true that I can't wear anything. I still feel cold in the winter, hot in the summer. I still don't particularly love getting caught in the rain, drops sizzling on my shoulders and face.

I order my clothing from labs that deal with corrosive acids. I wear protective gloves when I have to do computer work or make meals.

When no one's around, though, I leave my body bare and lethal. I stand in front of the mirror, running my hands over arms and legs no one else can touch.

My hair fell out before my thirteenth birthday. My parents thought I would cry, but I liked myself better bald, my scalp shining defiant. I pierced my ears and my nose later that year. Steel holds up well to acid skin.

When people look at me, they don't realize how dangerous I am. I think it's because we've spent too long in cities, using words and clothes to communicate instead of skin. If they looked close, if they imagined themselves in a rainforest—where colors, sheen, toxins are everything—they could know. It's not like I keep it a secret.

It would mean nothing if no one knew.

My skin is slightly reflective, acid secreting from my pores. I look hydrated, beautiful in deadliness. Makeups melt off. I hardly ever bothered with it anyway.

My parents call it a shame. I grew up hearing about a cousin who sold her soul for beauty only to take her life a year later. She was meant to be an example, they said. But how could her choice ever compare to mine?

They'll never understand why I did this. They say I threw away my future, any chance at giving them grandchildren.

They don't realize that I never intended to have sex. I never intended to care for anything but me.

On the train, my acid skin shimmers under fluorescent lights. It's a warning, like the unrestrained colors of a poison dart frog.

But the predators around me don't see it. They don't pay attention to the danger signs.

When I asked for my skin I imagined thorns, spikes. Some days I wish I'd been more specific. Maybe if my danger was more visible, they'd leave me alone. And yet I'm not sure even those warnings would be heeded.

Anyway, acid is better.

I was eleven when it started. I hadn't gotten my period or even boobs big enough to fill a training bra. What's it training us for? I used to wonder. Why's it got bows, lace, sequins? I hated the way it mixed childhood and sex, conflated cuteness with invitation. I never wore a bra then, or since.

Walking with my parents on the street, but too far behind. Enough to attract a man in a truck—windows rolled down and a comment tossed out onto the breeze as I crossed the road. Take your time baby, take your time.

I never saw his face. Turning too late, I only saw the anonymous truck driving away, too fast and too slow.

I should've been angry, furious. But I wasn't. I was embarrassed. Confused. I felt stupid, naive, scared. I blamed myself for falling behind, for being ten feet into being alone.

I could see my parents ahead, just on the other side of the road, close enough that if he'd spoken a little louder, they might have heard. Even if they had, I know what they would've said.

Oh, you're becoming a lady now, my father would've laughed.

We'll have a talk later, my mother would've said. About the difference between men and boys.

They didn't hear, though. The truck drove away, and I ran to them, chasing my childhood in their wake. But to my horror, it didn't fit me anymore. My body didn't feel like it belonged to me anymore.

From one side of the street to another, I'd lost my grip on it. I would never have it back.

———◄O►———

The man across the train car ignores my shining skin. Or maybe it attracts him, lures him from one side to the other. The train lurches and he sways against me, his coat sizzling a warning.

How does he miss it? The scent of corroding cloth, my shimmer dripping down my cheeks, my arms. They never pay attention to what's important. They don't sense the danger.

I let it slide until he reaches for my back, fingers creeping down, down over my reinforced jeans.

I snatch his hand, squeeze before releasing it.

His screams fill the car. Blood drips onto the floor as the flesh of his palm curls back, his nerves exposed to the air. Muscles dissolve, veins break into wet pools of burst cells. I pivot into the corner of the car, my hands leaving singed prints on the grab handle. I grin at the sight of bone, polished white by my acid touch. Somebody presses the emergency button. The man is yelling obscenities at me now as if it's my fault, as if I forced him to touch me.

It's always me. Never him.

He's helped off at the next stop, still bleeding. I regret not slapping him, soaking his face in acid as well. Losing a hand isn't enough.

The doors slide closed on a smear of red, the car quiet once more. We lurch forward and I close my eyes, counting the stations left before mine.

I hope his bones dissolve, forever revoking his ability to touch.

———•◦•———

The train cultivated them—grew predators on every car like weeds. Leaning in, touching me. Murmured comments trailed me home from school, made me jump at corners and shadows. I begged my mom to pick me up in her car, but she said it was too far, didn't work with her schedule, and besides, my parents were paying for my Charlie Card. Most teenagers would love to have that kind of independence.

A week before my first period, a man grabbed my hip, shoved his hard-on against me.

You look so lost, another laughed, showing too many teeth.

Need help getting home? I can give you a lift.

Another made lewd motions it took me months to understand.

No one stopped them. Faces turned down, gazes averted as if this was normal. Every day I tried to secure a seat early, sitting beside other women. But I was too young. Looks shot my way when I refused to give up my seat to older people, people laden with bags and babies. Courtesy demanded I get up, stand with the men, one hand white-knuckled around the grab handle, useless for defending myself.

When I gave up my seat, my protection, they thanked me. If only I'd been able to spit acid in their pleasant, blameless faces.

"What about partners?" my friends always ask. They want to meet at bars, go to clubs. I could come along, cover myself up and pretend to like the gazes on my glistening scalp.

I don't intend to end up alone. I love talking. I love sharing interests. I can have all the partners I want without being touched. Without touching back.

Maybe eventually, they'll understand. And if not ... I can walk away. I can walk away, and not worry about who's walking behind.

I turned twenty today.

It's been eight years since I've been hugged. Eight years since I've been kissed. Eight years since someone held my hand for longer than it takes to feel their skin melt away.

In my dorm room, I make a circle out of pens, textbooks, three bags of Sun Chips, and my Diva cup. I draw sigils from memory, using charcoal from my art supplies. I sit back, adjusting my gloves.

My daimon arrives as quickly as before. Xe looks the same, xyr tails twisting together, xyr eyes blinking without emotion.

"I'm surprised," xe says. Xyr voice has changed. It sounds older, like mine.

I tug my gloves off, freeing my shimmering hands. I adjust my septum ring, run my fingers over my scalp. Acid hydrates my palms. "Why are you surprised? You made me like this."

Xe nods. "I remember well, Kahlia. I'm surprised that you called me back."

"Why?"

"Because you have no regret."

I breathe in. Out. My tongue is moist, my heartbeat steady. I look down at my body, naked and dangerous and lovely.

"No. I don't."

"Then why am I here?"

I look at xem. Xyr body—strong, complex, untouchable within the circle I made. I run my hands over my arms, legs, torso. I feel my skin, protecting me for eight years. Protecting me better than half-baked warnings and well meaning advice ever did.

"I called you because I wanted to thank you." I rest my hands in my shining lap. "You made me brave."

Xe looks at me with xyr uncountable eyes. "You think so?"

I frown. "What?"

My daimon creeps up to the edge of the circle. Our gazes are level, xyr breath just touching my corrosive face. "You really think I was the one who made you brave?"

The Guest Room

R.L. Meza

As the car pulled out of the driveway before dawn, Eddy promised there would be no more *episodes*. He promised again at the restaurant where they stopped to eat lunch, halfway to Grandma's house. And again out front, as Dad parked between Uncle Fred's beat-up work truck and Aunt Sandra's shiny new Suburban—pinkie swore, in fact. *Episodes* was the word Eddy's mother used, instead of *fits* or *meltdowns*. As if Eddy's life was one of her soap operas.

His last *episode* ruined Christmas. Little Eddy's panicked howls had woken everyone staying over at Grandma's. He even wet the bed. His parents had stuck him in one of the guest bedrooms on the second floor, insisting Eddy was old enough to sleep alone. They'd given him a choice between the room with the nutcracker statue, or the one with Grandma's antique clowns.

Little Eddy was no dummy—or so he'd thought. He'd taken one look at the rows of painted porcelain faces, the silky stripes and spots, and darted straight into the nutcracker room. It was a simple matter of odds. Eddy figured he'd rather fight off one nutcracker on Christmas Eve than a whole army of creepy clowns.

He was wrong.

The nutcracker stood right beside the door, between the bed and Eddy's escape. It was life-sized—a giant to seven-year-old Eddy, who was already small for his age.

Exhausted from the long drive, Eddy fell asleep right away. He snored softly, drooling on the pillow, until the clacking of the nutcracker's wooden jaws startled him awake. He didn't know where he was, didn't recognize the frilly lace curtains covering the window, couldn't understand how the window had swapped walls with his own bedroom door. Where were his posters? His Star Wars bedsheets were gone, replaced by a comforter that smelled like crumbly potpourri. By the time Eddy remembered where he was, it was too late.

He gawked at the blank space beside the door.

The nutcracker was missing.

And poor Eddy, little dummy that he was, had left his hand dangling over the edge of the bed while he slept. From under the bedskirt, the nutcracker's fuzzy hat rose into view, a shadow climbing from the floor, and Eddy felt wooden jaws snap shut on his fingertips.

His bladder let go and he screamed. He kept on screaming until his mother shook him awake in the hall. Slammed his fingers in the door while sleepwalking, Dad explained. Apologizing to the disgruntled family members rubbing their eyes and grumbling about three o'clock in the morning.

Night terrors.

Nobody griped about the adopted kid wrecking his first family Christmas out loud, but still. Eddy felt their resentment. He'd seen how tired and grouchy everyone was, yawning as they tore open presents on Christmas morning.

<hr />

But this summer visit was a Big Deal. This was the annual family reunion—Eddy's first—and he was determined not to screw it up.

When they gave Eddy his choice of guest rooms, he marched right into the one with the nutcracker. He was a Big Boy now. When his mother suggested they move it to the closet, he just laughed—never mind the fear loosening his bowels. He would make his parents proud. Prove he belonged.

No more *episodes.*

So when the doorknob turned, and the strange lady poked her head in, Eddy believed her that the house was too crowded and they'd have to share a room. Family members were still pouring in from all over the country. Eddy heard the doorbell's persistent chiming below, the dull murmur of greetings and conversation drifting up through the floor.

Overwhelmed by the rush of new faces, he'd gone to bed early. Besides, his face hurt from smiling. He was tired of being hugged by grownups he'd never seen before. Sick of being prodded into family pictures that took forever, because the adults wanted everyone arranged by height, but the youngest cousins couldn't sit still, and people of different heights kept arriving, so then they had to start all over. He was sick *and* tired of listening to forced laughter from one side of the family, while shrinking from the scowls of the other half, thanks to Uncle Fred's tasteless jokes. Eddy just wanted to sleep.

He had already survived a parade of strangers. What was one more?

Eddy sure as heck wasn't going to bother his parents by complaining. Mom was asleep in the next room with a migraine. Dad was out in the yard, doing what he called *hard-earned relaxin'* with the other uncle-brother-grandpa-cousins. Standing around the fire pit with beers in hand, while the grandma-cousin-sister-aunts prepared tomorrow's feast in the kitchen. Eddy was pretty sure that was *sexist*—that's the word his mother used, but only ever *after* they'd returned home from a family event. While she was at Grandma's, Mom smiled just as wide as everyone else. Like it was a competition she wanted to win.

Eddy thought it was weird that the strange lady didn't use the bathroom to change into her pajamas. He tried not to peek—Eddy wasn't a *pre-vert*, or anything—but the wet popping sounds made him curious. She had her back to him, facing the long oval mirror in the corner. When her spine rippled, Eddy nearly bit through his tongue. He focused on the nutcracker, instead.

Another *night terror*.

He was having a nightmare; the lady probably wasn't even *real*.

Eddy pinched his arm. It hurt like heck, but he wasn't going to scream. He would not embarrass his parents again. He'd pinkie swore.

Besides, if she was real, she was family. She had to be.

The lady unzipped her massive suitcase and began transferring its contents to the closet. She had a Mary Poppins amount of stuff in her bag. Eddy tried to guess what the objects were by the sounds they made—clinking metal, swishing fabric, a dry rattle—but he couldn't. When he mustered the courage to look, the closet door was already closed, the suitcase hidden from view.

The lady had vanished like a ghost.

Eddy yelped as the mattress tilted behind him, threatening to roll him to the center. Like the nutcracker, the lady had moved—except, no, that had been a *night terror*. This was reality and Eddy was eight years old, a Big Boy. All he had to do was prove it.

Keep quiet.

No more *episodes*.

Do. Not. Ruin. The. Family. Reunion.

Still, Eddy thought it was even weirder that the lady didn't offer to sleep on the floor, or ask him to. The bed was a twin. The plastic mattress protector Grandma had covered it with rustled every time she moved.

And the lady moved A LOT.

She didn't touch him, not once. But Eddy couldn't sleep. His skin crawled. He had a funny feeling, like she was staring at the back of his head in the dark. The thought of her watching stiffened his muscles, making it impossible for him to relax. The hairs on the back of his neck stood erect like tiny sensors, waiting for the tickling brush of contact. Every time he started to drift off, the lady moved again, and he went rigid, dreading the moment she would tire of watching and finally reach out to touch him.

Before the sun came up, the lady was out of bed. She stood before the mirror, naked. As Eddy watched through cracked eyelids, the strange lady shrank a few inches. She pulled objects from the closet—dim outlines—and put herself together.

Eddy looked for the lady at breakfast. Everyone was up early, even the kids, forming a line that curved past the buffet of scrambled eggs, greasy meats, and pancakes. As Eddy followed the line winding back through the dining room, between the pair of long adult tables, to the trio of kids' tables set up with folding chairs, he realized he couldn't remember the names of half these people, let alone their faces. Anxiety clawed at his ribs like a caged bear.

Eddy's stomach flopped and rolled at the sight of his grinning cousins, their faces smeared with ketchup and syrup. Their screeching pierced his ears. Eddy quivered, spilling orange juice all over the carpet.

He didn't want to sit, but he did. He sure as heck didn't feel like eating, not with so many grownups looking down from their higher tables, barking at his cousins to mind their manners, clean their plates.

Going on about eyes bigger than stomachs.

Uncle So-and-So clapped Eddy on the back, then squeezed Eddy's shoulders. The greeting made Eddy uncomfortable—too intimate, too familiar for a guy he'd just met twelve hours ago. But Eddy smiled and said, sure he'd like more orange juice. And sorry about the mess. When Eddy's mother finally appeared amid the others, he nearly wept with relief.

Since Eddy couldn't pinpoint the strange lady by sight, he tried to locate her by sound. But hungry cousins make A LOT of icky-wet noises—especially the toddlers, chewing with their mouths open. Every pop made Eddy jump and spin around. Uncle Fred, twisting in his chair to crack his back. Or What's-her-face, with the black lipstick and chipped black fingernails, popping her knuckles one by one to gross out the younger cousins. By the time the dining room was almost empty, Eddy was no closer to identifying the strange lady.

He looked down at his plate, dismal. Nauseous, Eddy filled his mouth. Chewed. Swallowed. Again and again. The house rule was you couldn't leave the table until your plate was empty. Breakfast was a lump in his gut.

Someone leaned over Eddy's left shoulder and told him to *finish it*. Just the two words, but Eddy knew who it was. The strange lady.

His breakfast came up fast, half-chewed, spurting over the tablecloth.

Her height was average. The strange lady's face was narrow, her features plain. As he wiped his mouth with the back of his hand, Eddy tried to commit it to memory.

But she could have been anyone.

Brown hair, like most of the women in his family. Brown eyes. Eddy turned his attention to her clothes: a long, patterned dress that hung past her ankles, modest flats on her feet.

But clothing could be changed, often and easily.

Eddy looked around for his parents. The dining room was vacant, except for the lady. Her breathing was thick and moist, heavy with mucus, catching as she hovered behind Eddy. He wished she'd clear her throat. He tried to mop up his mess with a napkin before anyone noticed, but then one of the nameless girls came running in, chased by a boy Eddy barely knew.

She took one look at Eddy's puke and upchucked down the front of her overalls. Started crying. The boy turned green, too.

Eddy fled as the girl's wailing drew random adults to the dining room. He would just have to hope the cousins couldn't remember his name either, so they wouldn't be able to blame him. But when Eddy cast a look back, he saw the strange lady whispering to his mother, who then turned toward him.

The strange lady winked.

Eddy asked his mother about her later, while the cousins played freeze-tag on the lawn and the adults milled around the barbecues. He pointed to the fruit trees fringing the yard, where the strange lady sat in the shade, sipping lemonade. Her posture was stiff, her eyes obscured by large sunglasses. Whenever a cousin ran past, her head swiveled to track the motion before slowly turning back toward Eddy.

Eddy's mother hummed. "I don't know who she is," she said. "You'll have to ask your father."

But when Eddy asked his father, Dad told him she was probably Uncle Fred's new girlfriend. That, or maybe the wife of one of the second cousins—whatever the heck *that* meant—flown in from Georgia. He told Eddy to man up and ask her himself.

No. Freaking. Way. Eddy couldn't talk to her. His throat dried up at the thought, pasted shut, like he'd guzzled a tube of super glue.

Eddy spent the rest of the day watching his cousins leap, shrieking, into the pool. Sweat trickled down his back, soaking his shirt. He wanted to swim, but that meant changing into his bathing suit.

And his bathing suit was in the guest room. All the way upstairs.

Eddy didn't want to bump into the strange lady again, if he could help it. He thought about asking his parents to let him sleep in their room, but after the scene at breakfast, Eddy was too embarrassed. He was afraid the strange lady would turn everyone against him. They all seemed to really like her. Yet, no matter how intently Eddy eavesdropped, he never caught his relatives using her name.

Not once.

Grandma couldn't remember who the strange lady was. She told Eddy to ask his mother.

So he was back to square one.

———— ◄O► ————

Eyes screwed shut, knees tucked to his chest, Eddy tried to keep still while the strange lady climbed into bed behind him.

He pinched himself repeatedly as he struggled to stay awake. But after a day spent pretending to be brave—the perfect son-cousin-grandkid—exhaustion dragged him into a fitful sleep.

In the middle of the night, Eddy woke. Without thinking, he rolled over. His forearm smacked something solid.

It was the nutcracker, lying beside him.

Beneath the blankets, he saw that the statue was stripped down. Polished wood gleamed in the moonlight filtering between the curtains. The nutcracker's arms were stiff, wide painted eyes fixed on the ceiling.

Slowly, dreamlike, Eddy rolled toward the door. Saw the tall, fuzzy hat. The uniform.

The new nutcracker was shorter, slimmer. As it approached the bed, he scrambled backward, but his escape was blocked by the naked wooden body of the old nutcracker. Trapped between the two, his bladder grew hot. Warmth stained the sheets in a rush. Eddy's heart was pounding out of his chest, but all he could think was: *I did it again. Another episode. The visit is ruined.*

Beneath the fuzzy hat, the strange lady pressed a finger to the red slit of her mouth. Her face was a pale blur, an out-of-focus moon, filling Eddy's vision as she bent over the bed. Her voice had changed. Soft and papery, like insect wings.

"Shh," the strange lady said. Her breath was cold. "If you're quiet, if you're very still, I'll change the bed when I'm finished. No one needs to know."

Eddy almost screamed for his mother then. But tomorrow was the last day—the night of The Big Family Dinner—and he knew his parents would be disappointed if they were forced to drive home early. They might take away his toys as punishment. Or, worse—they might rethink the adoption. Eddy closed his eyes as the room started to spin.

Yes, they would decide that Eddy and his *episodes* weren't worth the trouble. They had signed papers. Eddy knew how receipts worked. If something wasn't working right, you returned it. Got a different one.

So Eddy kept his eyes closed while the strange lady pressed the hard angles of her face to his, clicking and clacking.

Tugged on his skin, as if his cheeks were made of clay.

Unrolled something the length of his body.

Eddy heard the snick of scissors and flinched. But the lady did not touch him again. She didn't tell him she was finished either. Scared to move, Eddy listened to her footsteps fade across the carpet. Hinges squeaked. He heard the lady unzip her suitcase. The hinges squeaked again.

Finally, Eddy peeked. An eerie blue-green glow emanated from between the slats of the closet door. No sign of the strange lady or her oversized bag. She must be in there.

Eddy slipped out of bed, crept out of the guest room.

His mother found him sleeping in the bathtub the next morning. Eddy lied, said he was feeling sick—something he ate, probably.

"Oh," his mother said. Her face fell. "If you're sick, we should go home early."

"No!" Eddy said, a bit too loud. He insisted on returning to his room alone, to change his clothes himself. His mother raised an eyebrow, but didn't argue. She seemed relieved, even. Eddy was growing up, becoming more responsible.

Really, he just wanted to make sure she wouldn't see the soiled bedsheets.

But the bedding was crisp and clean, like the strange lady had promised.

Eddy longed to open the closet and investigate the suitcase stowed inside, but he'd seen the way the strange lady had tattled on him for puking. If she was still in the closet, or if she caught him, she would certainly tell Eddy's mother. Everyone would know he was snooping. They would think he was a sneak—a *pre-vert*.

Eddy didn't need to search for the strange woman at breakfast. She sat down right beside him. She was even smaller now—young enough to sit at the kids' table. None of Eddy's relatives seemed to notice the oddly somber girl among them. Lank blonde hair, eyes muddy brown. She wore a pink shirt and blue jeans, the same style of canvas sneakers the other kids favored. Also pink. Around one wrist hung a bracelet like the ones the cousins had made at the crafts table the night before. Plastic beads in bright colors. Eddy squinted, trying to make out the lettering on the white beads that spelled out her name. But the letters were symbols—a language Eddy couldn't speak. Maybe if he held his tongue and gargled, he'd come close to saying it right.

None of the grownups could tell him who the strange girl was. They simply shrugged and pointed Eddy toward a different family. Everyone was too pre-occupied with cooking for The Big Dinner or *relaxin'*, or settling squabbles between the cousins, to humor Eddy's questions. Especially since she had a habit of disappearing when the adults were paying attention. She was somebody's kid or sister or cousin, surely.

She wouldn't be here, otherwise—eh, Eddy?

More photos. More smiling. More hugging.

By dinnertime, Eddy was a nervous wreck. Every counter in his grandmother's expansive kitchen was covered with steaming, fragrant dishes. He added a single bread roll to his plate, and when the last crumb was finished, he leaned toward the adult tables and squeaked, "Can I be excused?"

No one heard him over the roar of conversation, the clink of silverware on plates, the noisy chewing. The tables were laden with food and elbows, the chairs set close enough that everyone was rubbing shoulders, squeezed together like cattle at a feeding trough. All the members of Eddy's family were present now, talking excitedly between bites. Catching up, making plans for the future, laughing. Not one of them was listening to Eddy.

He tried again, louder, singling out his father in the chaos. "Dad, can I be excused?"

"*May* I be excused," Eddy's father corrected. His mother added, "Say please, Eddy."

Eddy made the necessary adjustments. "*May* I be excused, *please*?"

The grownups' heads bobbed in approval.

Eddy gave his mother an obligatory peck on the cheek before scurrying from the dining room. It felt rude to leave his plate in the dirty pile beside the sink for his aunts to wash—they'd done all the cooking, after all—so Eddy scrubbed his plate with his shirt and set the dish on the clean pile. Now no one could accuse him of being sloppy. After a final glance at the dining room, Eddy snuck upstairs.

He needed to know what was inside the strange lady's suitcase. Now was his only chance, while she was busy stuffing her cheeks full of Grandma's strawberry shortcake. Eddy threw the closet door open and knelt beside the suitcase, tugged on the zipper.

Eddy was hoping for a purse like his mother's, with a wallet inside. He wasn't a thief. He just wanted to check the lady's I.D. to find out whose family she'd come with.

What Eddy found instead was a perfect replica of himself.

A segmented arm curled around second-Eddy's chest. Too many fingers encircled his throat—Eddy lost count at nine. Clammy skin hugged him close. Scales rasped against his earlobe as he felt the strange lady behind him, whispering something garbled in his ear, like one of Dad's old vinyl records played in reverse.

Pain pricked Eddy's neck, and all he could think was: *She stung me. Like a wasp.*

Numbness chased the pain away. All strength ran out from Eddy's muscles. He slumped, limp, to the floor. As his vision dwindled to a pinprick, he wondered how much time would pass before someone thought to look for him. There were so many cousins—would anyone even notice he was gone?

Or would they scrunch up their faces and say, "Who?"

Eddy's tongue wouldn't obey. He panted through his nostrils as the lady unloaded her suitcase, then repacked it. She placed Eddy inside, folding his limbs to fit. The zipper closed around him. The walls of the suitcase pressed in from all sides. He managed a pathetic whimper, low in his throat. He should've screamed when he had the chance—turned an *episode* into a full-length movie, so the grownups would *have* to pay attention.

Didn't they realize a stranger was among them?

Eddy counted the steps as the suitcase bumped down Grandma's stairs. His final coherent thought, this side of the reality he knew and understood was that the strange lady must have changed again. Her footsteps were sharp and loud—not kids' sneakers, but the click of high heels.

Or hooves, perhaps.

As the wheels of the suitcase purred along the cement walkway, Eddy lost consciousness. He did not hear the trunk close. He did not feel the engine start. He did not sense reality bending around him, curling and twisting like a nightmare. Like a *night terror*.

The strange lady raised her hand in a parting wave.

"Who's that fine piece of ass?" Uncle Fred said, as he returned the wave.

Exhaling a cloud of cigarette smoke into the driveway, Eddy's dad shrugged. "Beats me. I thought she came with you."

Echthroxenia

Avra Margariti

The man born and raised in my night terrors sits at our kitchen table, nibbling on rose loukoumia and sipping honey-sweetened tea. Grandma never takes my dowry tea set out of its hope chest unless we're hosting a special guest. The animal-bone teacup shrieks against the petal-painted saucer like grinding teeth; blooms and thorns transform in a vertiginous blur as the teacup meanders meridians from mouth, to saucer, and back again.

Pinching myself awake is not enough. I bite the inside of my cheek, hard enough to draw red blood from the pink flesh.

"Yiayia, what are you doing?" My voice unhinges, more hiss than whisper. I pull Grandma aside in the foyer full of ivory doilies and porcelain kitten figurines. All part of my proika, my bundle of small riches crafted or collected by generations of toiling women. Meant, not for me, but for my future husband to know my worth. "This man is ..."

But I don't know who—*what*—this man is. If, indeed, they are man, or beast, or shadow. Did they spring out of my nightmares, or have they been haunting me there in preparation for this meeting?

All I know is this apparition has followed me in sleep since I came to live with Grandma as an orphan. And now he's in our kitchen, slurping mountain tea with a twisting red tongue. His upper lip is dusted in sugar that sticks to every open pore, calderas defined in loose off-white that has bile crawling up my throat.

It's as if my eyes are somehow unable to absorb the entirety of his visage. Whenever I attempt to piece our guest's features together, my mind is lost in a haze of fog. All I can do is focus on these small details: the pitch-black of twin empty wells inside his eyes, the too-perfectly positioned edges of his hairline.

Grandma's clawed fingers around my wrist are an unspoken warning. "Don't be rude, Xenia. This man is a guest. We cannot afford to be unwelcoming and break the ancient rules of hospitality. The gods are always watching, waiting for us to slip up."

I wither under Grandma's stare piercing me through the wrinkled apertures of her eyes. Her disappointment drips sludge-like shame through my bloodstream. I stand alone in the foyer while she goes to take care of our guest.

My mouth tastes of blood and roses. All around me, porcelain kittens titter dainty taunts.

<hr />

Grandma is laughing, ladling vegetable soup. I have never seen her so full of vitality and easy charm since I came to live with her after my parents crashed and burned their business, relationship, car, lives.

Our guest lifts his bowl—eager but polite—to help direct the soup inside the dish's cavernous cradle. The globules that slip down the soupiere glint grotesquely in the candlelight, like egg sacs of some alien insect. I can only glance at his face from the corner of my eye. Every time I do, an eddy of mist takes his features away only to remake them infinitesimally different on the next uncanny swirl.

Yet his smile is straight and uniform, little gravestones arranged in a country cemetery, white as tea-stained doves.

"I'm so glad you're here at last! I was worried about Xenia being left on the shelf forever," Grandma confesses to our special guest, although I'm right there in the dining room. "She was beginning to look past her prime. Almost ..." Her voice lowers even further as if to cushion the scandal. "Almost like a *man*."

I look down at my plain trousers, torn and stained at the knees. They displease Grandma, who lays a different dress on my bed each morning, all embroidered sleeves, lace hems, crocheted collars. Mom's relics. I pinch and bite at myself again, wanting to see if I'm real or ghost—is he the dreamling, or am I?

Not a bite of roasted lamb passes through my constricting throat. I let Grandma chatter about our family—tragic deaths and modest inheritance—the town gossip, how all her friends are dead but she's so happy he's here. I wonder if some deceit-woven glamour has Grandma convinced he's an aspiring groom sent by the local proxenitra to ask for my hand in marriage, and not a creature prowling my every night terror. When she asks our guest questions, all I can hear of his words is static slicing through my eardrums. Yet his answers, always with that polite porcelain-smile, seem to satisfy Grandma throughout lunch.

When our guest offers to bring the dirty dishes back to the kitchen, Grandma pushes me in after him. Her smile is knowing, a barbed glint that commands: go help our guest who so selflessly offers his assistance.

In the kitchen, over the sound of water distending the leftovers in the sink, I swallow my revulsion enough to corner our ghost.

"Who are you?" I hiss while he, automaton-stiff, scrubs dishes, his suit cuffs raised to reveal skin that looks peculiarly breakable. His veins are cracks traversing pallid, almost transparent, forearms. I think I recognize the suit jacket as the one that once belonged to my father, moth-eaten now that its former wearer is food for the earthworms. "What do you want from me?" I try again.

The formal smile he offers is a marionette's moue, a tragedy mask's facade.

On closer inspection—through the buffer of a silver spoon's reflection, the kitchen windowpane, the row of Grandma's jarred preserves—he looks even more artificial, and familiar. A spiteful trick of the light, I tell myself.

Yet I can't stop staring at all our many reflections around the room. For a second suspended evermore through the ether, I cannot tell us apart. Until he's gone from my side and I'm left blinking at an empty, spotless kitchen.

———◇———

The baklava squelches sweet and syrupy like blood just beginning to congeal as the baked Greek coffee, dark and midnight-thick, stains our cups. The foam bubbles stare at me: all-seeing, all-knowing eyes. I'm too scared to drain my cup and face my fate foretold in the dregs.

The gramophone plays an old tune—*What is this thing called love?*—and I sway, in hypnotized place, weary down to my bones now that the day's adrenaline is catching up to me.

Grandma has seated us in the formal parlor, the one meant for special visitors. The couch's carved wooden back digs into my spine with every breath that shudders in and out of my lungs. She sits across from us, fiddling with the tarnished gramophone as our guest and I share the faded floral couch. The cushion space between us is not large enough to hide the way baklava-sweet bile claws up my esophagus.

Grandma's inane chatter mingles with the music. When I blink again, the light has changed from amber-tinged ambience to a crepuscular dimness. The visitors' parlor has vanished like an illusionist's act. Music still drifts distorted from somewhere I can't reach and so does Grandma's disembodied voice, while the walls tower tall, closing in on me.

I'm in a box, I think. *A coffin.*

"Your hope chest," my unleaving guest politely offers.

I whirl toward his voice, devoid of static here in this shared dreamscape, but echoing manifold. I know by sternum-rooted instinct that he's right. He and I have shifted to the inside of the heavy compact chest, its wooden slats smelling like an old ship's hold although it's lived in Grandma's house as many years as I have. The chest holds my proika, a heritage of sweat-drenched toil and tearful expectation.

I study, like a cornered animal, this cavernous dark space. Grandma is gone, and only my ghost and I remain. All around flit shadows cast by strange objects, every sound amplified against curved walls. Every breath, a shout.

Doilies hang on meat hooks like animal skins or—for the gauziest, flimsiest lace—sausage casings. Although in reality I know them to be no bigger than my cupped palms, these crocheted creations stretch large enough to be medieval castle tapestries depicting beheadings and deflowerings. They flap ghostly in the must-imbued drafts, shrouding my senses. The rose-patterned teacups and porcelain saucers are as vast as hills and lakes iced over. Sleeping beasts hide beneath the frost, dream-clamoring to strangle me with their talons, tentacles, and prehensile tongues. All my dead family's hopes and aspirations, all the proof of me as more property and price tag than person—everything grows swollen and suffocating.

And in the midst of it all, my ghost and I, standing one before the other like a mirror image I still cannot face head-on.

I laugh then, bitterness unfettered across this nuptial nightmarescape. We've been here before, I know this with the certainty of the doomed and the dreaming.

"This hope chest isn't mine," I say, choking on my laughter like a lace-braided noose. "This is what my ancestors bequeathed me, but not for me to start a life of my own. My fate is to forever polish silverware and weave linens like cobwebs to trap new daughters in old cycles."

I look at him: a hazy, ever-shifting vision. He is a guest in this house, and I'm a guest in my body. My gaze gravitates to the bone-gleaming teacups and the lace doilies like undulating waves of trypophobia-trigger seafoam. If only I could grasp them in my hands, these fragile treasures, if only I could lift them high above my head and—

I awaken with a jolt, still in the orange-lit visitors' parlor. The baklava effluvia stick resin-like to my fork tines, the coffee long gone cold, its dregs writhing with bleak visions.

Grandma frowns her disapproval for my daring to break decorum. For being who I have always been. "Now is no time to sleep," she chastises. "Come, come, you have work to do."

Day drags its carcass into night. Beyond the yellowed curtains, darkness spreads the way of viscous tar. Soon it will engulf us all: Grandma, our guest, and me. The walls and windows will close over jagged as petrified wounds, and only a hopeless chest will remain of this house. Only a coffin.

"Stop daydreaming," Grandma tuts, pulling me away from the window, glass spiderwebbed by my uneven breaths. "It's time to bring our guest his nightcap."

I had thought by now, meal after rich meal, the man who is not a man would have donned a heirloom hat and been on his ghostly way. Yet there he is, ensconced in the guest bedroom between my dowry's good linens—white as a wedding veil—that Grandma had me lay out for him earlier.

I take the amber glass of Metaxa liquor, letting myself be pushed toward the guest bedroom—an inexorable death march.

"Wait," I protest, although she always found my words most feeble. But maybe if I call upon etiquette, she will listen. "Yiayia, surely you don't mean I take the drink to his room by myself?"

Grandma's face appears more inscrutable than ever, wrinkles like nail-scratched wood, mouth an axe-slash across her weathered face. "Remember, Xenia, you're not getting any younger. Sometimes the way to secure a man is to leave him no choice but to do the right thing."

My skin pales and pebbles with shivers. So she wants me in his bed, though unwed. Wants me to perform the old-wives' trick of getting pregnant with child, wrapping a ring around this stranger's finger. Sweeping myself out of Grandma's hair at last. Straight into the arms of an apparition.

Xenia—the ancient custom of hospitality after which I was named—states that once you've clothed, fed, and entertained your guest, offered them a roof over their head, you must give the guest a parting gift as well. A frenzied giggle escapes me as I realize I am to be that gift.

Darkness embraces the guest bedroom, a mockery of a wedding suite. I fumble my way toward the wispy, immaterial shape stretched out on the mattress. My hope chest stands at the foot of the bed that isn't mine. The fruits of my lineage's sweat and tears, blood drawn from embroidery needles—I am not worthy of it all, this much has been made clear. Yet whatever stranger lays his head here is deserving of the contents of my proika.

I lie in bed on my side, me and my apparition facing each other. For the first time since he arrived, I force myself to truly look at him. I try to make out the details of his silhouette, push through foggy features and roiling nausea, to the meat of him underneath.

He has my face, like I pulled him out of my innermost matter, made him in my image from dream clay and bone china. And he is docile, the way it was expected of me to be, first by my parents, then Grandma.

"Why are you here?" I whisper. When I raise my hand toward his face, his hand mirrors mine—puppet and puppeteer.

"Why am I here?" the stranger asks.

"Did I summon you?" I try again.

"Did you summon me?" he replies, voice rumbling wet and distant. A mud-made thing. I devour my disgust for my fingers to finally make contact with his face. When his own touch meets my skin, it is cold, sleek, lifeless.

"You are an empty man," I speak into the darkness.

"I am an empty man," the darkness replies.

As soon as they are uttered, I know the words to be true. The world once more rearranges itself, the way every atom of reality did in my dreams.

This mannequin of a man is nothing but a vessel for my freedom. My sleeping mind knew Grandma would never grant me access to my dowry without a husband by my side, to accompany me, lead me through life. So I molded a glamour out of my night terrors. An empty man that used to disgust me so, now standing before me, still and obedient. Awaiting my direction.

All day long—and all my days before that—I have been a polite, gracious host. A polite, gracious orphan. *Be thankful Grandma took you in after your parents' deaths. Marry well to repay her kindness, crochet more doilies with cramping, aching fingers, stop crying, Xenia, you will grow ugly, as ugly as a man, nobody will want you then. Nobody will ever want you.*

Was it any wonder my dream-self manifested us a trick husband, a ghost decoy? And if I can mold an empty man, what else can I do?

I lie back in bed and weave my fingers in the air, working with the encircling dark, rather than against it.

"Well, husband?" I speak toward the ceiling. "What's mine is yours. Such are the ancient rules of hospitality. Matrimony, too. So *take it*."

I close my eyes, listening to the mattress shift as my apparition moves above me. He climbs off the bed, mechanical footsteps ambling toward the hope chest, old hinges creaking open through the resistance of rust.

I fall asleep to the sounds of porcelain shattering, silverware bending, and lace ripped to shreds. Never have I slept this deep, and sweeter than a baby.

See Something Say Something

Nadia Bulkin

Ashlyn had always been good at keeping secrets, and Bockscar was by far her biggest. Bigger than losing her virginity to Cody McDonald by the lake in ninth grade; bigger than cutting a hole in Ranae's wedding dress the night before the ceremony and blaming it on the seamstress. Bockscar was a secret to end all secrets.

The last secret that she, Ashlyn Jacobsen, would ever keep.

Bockscar did not understand how special secrets were to humans. When Pastor Delbert drove to the house at 8 a.m. on a Tuesday to warn Ashlyn's father that a demonic presence had fixed its sight on his family, Bockscar thought that Ashlyn ought to go ahead and reveal their relationship.

What's the worst that can happen? Bockscar asked, in a tone that made Ashlyn's lips curl.

A lot of bad things could happen if her family discovered she was talking to Bockscar. She was ready for some of them— having her phone taken away, being on bathroom duty for a year. She wasn't ready for the very worst, which she imagined to be institutionalization, and that was why she was sitting in the truck on Friday afternoon waiting for her cousin Steph to get off a cross-country bus. Because if anyone could take the fall for a demonic infestation, it was the city girl who'd been raised by a single mother on cigarettes and boxed mac and cheese.

The bus was late, so there was nothing for Ashlyn to do but lean on the steering wheel and admire the paint peeling off Victory Community Church across the street. Bockscar's influence, no doubt. Pastor Delbert loved to remind his flock of how long he'd been lording over his iron pulpit—twenty years this April—but Bockscar had been in that churchyard for over a century. To be fair, Bockscar kept a low profile. *I don't call anyone,* Bockscar once corrected her. *You call yourselves.* Even Ashlyn wouldn't have known that anything was in the well behind the church if she hadn't snuck out of fellowship to help Ruth Gaddie take pictures for some loser with a godly girl fetish.

Ruth Gaddie—whatever happened to that little heathen? Juvie? A baby? Ashlyn blinked, and Bockscar filled her eyes with the answer: a video camera in a bedroom, boxes of expensive clothes. Ashlyn's father always did say that by leaving the church the Gaddies had bought a one-way ticket to hell.

But look who was in hell now?

Well, maybe not quite *in* hell; maybe still skipping along the brimstone path. Pastor Delbert had all but said as much on Tuesday morning, claiming to have seen their house in a terrible dream: a small flat square sitting alone in a ring of red light, sinking into what he called a *fetid marsh.* He told her father to keep an eye on the women. The meat of the family, as Pastor Delbert put it, that hung off the bones of the men.

Bockscar said that Pastor Delbert was a self-hating sadist.

The 73 bus finally pulled in and a few miserable-looking people in faded souvenir sweatshirts stumbled off. Steph was last, crumpled beneath a large hiking backpack that made her look like a hermit crab. She'd cut her hair since her mother's funeral last year; it didn't look good.

Ashlyn gave the horn a couple taps, and Steph hurried over in what looked like relief. *She was afraid she wasn't actually talking to you,* Bockscar said. *She thought you'd been hacked.* Ashlyn giggled—or at least she thought she was the one doing the giggling. Sometimes with Bockscar sitting so close, it was hard to tell where she ended and Bockscar began.

Steph heaved herself into the cab with all the grace of a newborn calf.

"I like your hair, by the way," Ashlyn said. "Super cute."

"Oh, thanks." Steph's voice was raspy, tortured. "Yeah, nothing like having your mom drop dead to make you want to try a fresh new look."

Ashlyn hummed sympathetically. "The one good thing that happens when you lose everything is you get a chance to figure out who you really are. That's what Bockscar says, anyway."

"Who's Bockscar? Is that your boyfriend?"

Bockscar showed her what Steph was imagining—a bad boy on a motorcycle, promising weed and an escape to California or Mexico or Anywhere But Here. Ashlyn smiled, imagining Bockscar picking her up in a cloud of black smoke, promising to have her home before the apocalypse. "That's just what everyone calls him," she said, the lie slipping from her mouth so fast that it hardly seemed to be one. "He's got these awful acne scars on his cheek."

"Oh." The sun roared out from behind a cloud and Steph squinted to protect herself. "That's kinda mean."

"He doesn't mind. But don't tell anyone about him, okay? My dad thinks I'm gonna marry this goodie-goodie from church, Jared Hatch." She stuck her tongue out in disgust. Bockscar snickered, knowing she wasn't faking that reaction.

Steph grinned. It was the first time Ashlyn had seen her mouth curve that way. "My lips are sealed."

"Anyway, what about you? You must meet interesting guys in the city."

At that comment, Steph laughed outright. "Yeah, *interesting*. If you call married guys who don't mention they're married *interesting*."

Ashlyn pouted. "Oof, I'm sorry. Then maybe it's good for you to come spend some time with us. That's what we were thinking, anyway. We've always got your back."

Steph gave her an awkward look, probably because she wasn't accustomed to being invited to family gatherings. Or maybe she could sense that the family didn't actually want her to visit—given the stress of Pastor Delbert thinking they were slipping into a fetid marsh and all, Ashlyn had to beg. She said Steph was dying to get to know them and desperately in need of an escape from city life, but it wasn't until she said this was what Dead Aunt Bonnie would have wanted that her father relented. Aunt Bonnie had supposedly gone into the city many years ago to spread the word of God and fallen prey to the temptations of evil men. Ashlyn had always had doubts about that story, but in the Jacobsen house, her father's word was law.

At least, so he thought.

"Nice to be around *some* folks who think I'm cool, I guess," Steph muttered.

"Trust me," Ashlyn said. "Everyone is *so* excited to see you."

——◆——

With Bockscar, everything was illuminated. But with clarity came risk. Ashlyn had to be so watchful, all the time, to make sure she wasn't doing anything that was supposed to be out of reach— which was hard, considering her domain was limited to home economics. And while the demands of her faith had given her plenty of experience with concealment, she was still human. Some things—very few things—slipped.

Like when she accidentally revealed that she knew Jared Hatch was coming to dinner before anyone could tell her. Her father seemed pleased when she explained that she and Jared had been texting, but Ashlyn could tell from her stepmother's stormy expression that Ranae didn't buy it. Of course Ranae didn't believe her—a woman could always tell when another woman was faking. That was how Ashlyn had known, long before she met Bockscar, that Ranae had only married her father because Pastor Delbert told her to. Because she had no will of her own.

After that slip, Ashlyn needed a distraction. She elbowed Steph in the ribs. "Tell them about the crazy guy who got kicked off your bus," she said, knowing the family would be transfixed by a story of external menace and drug-fueled insanity. It was in their interest to believe the worst about the world, after all. Steph crunched her brow in confusion, but obliged.

She slipped again at dinner, while Jared was talking about his upcoming mission trip. He was going on and on about cross-cultural discipleship, looking especially sickly in his white button-down shirt, and she was wondering how long her soul would survive being Mrs. Jared Hatch when she was suddenly overcome by the sensation of a rubber hose pushing down her esophagus. She coughed; she dragged her tongue across the back of her throat; she stuck her fingers into her mouth and closed them around a small wet glob of flesh that did not belong to her—not yet, anyway. Sometimes she wondered if Bockscar intentionally sent her these violent sensations, violent images, in order to force her hand.

"Ashlyn, gross," Cousin Wyatt blurted from across the table. "What the heck are you doing?"

Ashlyn withdrew her hand and Aunt Bex reprimanded Wyatt for interrupting Jared, but it was too late—Ashlyn could see across the table that Ranae's chewing had slowed to a dull gnaw, like Kristaleigh Franklin grinding tiny bites of beans into a fine paste in order to slow down her swallowing.

She's thinking, Bockscar said. *She knows.*

Things hadn't gone well for Ranae the first and last time she tried to confront Ashlyn directly, over a sink of unwashed dishes. Ranae simply hadn't understood back then that Ashlyn knew exactly how to crumple at her father's feet, how to twist her mouth just so as she explained why *she* was the one he needed to protect. So this time Ranae tried something else. Something sneakier. She leaned over and whispered to Ashlyn's father that she needed to talk to him after dinner.

If only Ranae knew that there was no whisper quiet enough to escape Bockscar.

She's going to tell your father.

The thought let loose a primal fear within Ashlyn so loud and sharp that Bockscar must have heard it rattling around her bones—because suddenly the plates started rattling and the silverware started flying and when the mashed potatoes exploded in mid-air, everyone screamed.

At first Ashlyn didn't know why Bockscar was doing this. But as a knife flew across the table, she suddenly understood: the chaos broke the stillness of the dinner, gave her room to maneuver. It let Ashlyn duck under the table, crawl toward Ranae's denim-clad legs, and drag her off her chair—saving the woman from an airborne glass that would have cut her throat had she stayed at her seat. Bockscar would have made sure of it.

It wasn't that Ashlyn particularly cared for Ranae. She also wasn't particularly afraid of fountains of blood; Bockscar had shown her plenty in her sleep and she'd come to appreciate their warmth, the bubbling rush. It was what she knew followed the blood that she wasn't ready for: the void. The big empty. The dead air behind the billowing red theater curtain. Bockscar hadn't shown her that; she knew it was there.

And Bockscar loved her enough to give her the time she needed—time to repair her cover, to prepare for her future, to accustom herself to the idea that everyone in the family would find out about the two of them sooner or later. But not yet.

Ranae looked like a child under the table. She and her big dumb doe eyes were such a weak replacement for Ashlyn's mother; it would have felt almost pathetic to kill her.

"Thank you," Ranae panted, and as Bockscar took the ceiling light out with a whip of energy, she threw her arms around Ashlyn. Forgiving her for her years of rudeness and disrespect and out-and-out cruelty. Forgetting.

She would say nothing now to Ashlyn's father. Ashlyn had made sure of that.

⬥

Bockscar was in a mood on Saturday morning, waking Ashlyn up by opening her ballerina music box and lighting her favorite vanilla candle at 5a.m. The light was thin and the house was quiet and Bockscar had a tendency to stir into a tizzy after a big night.

She sat up, gently shut her music box, and carried the candle into the bathroom. She'd long ago learned the hard way that no one was going to have a good time if she ignored Bockscar.

You're going to back out, Bockscar said once she settled in the bathtub. *Even after everything you promised, you're going to keep telling me no. I don't want to spend the next seventy years playing poltergeist for a sky-pilot's housewife.*

Ashlyn cringed. This sort of talk reminded her of Cody McDonald, sulking with sticky hands by the lake. But she didn't fault Bockscar for this pushiness. Even Pastor Delbert's God was a jealous god.

I am not Cody, Bockscar reminded her, and flared the candle flame bright and big enough that she could see a pinprick version of herself pirouetting on the wick like a music box ballerina, cocooned by a wall of heat in the coolest part of the fire. This was the miracle of Bockscar's blessing. It reminded her of the divine light Pastor Delbert always talked about at church—all brilliance and power and the promise of a life that was something other than the bowels of a cave. She knew Bockscar's light wasn't the same—she wasn't stupid—but at least Bockscar's light was real. *I am the world.*

"Don't worry," she whispered, pulling the candle closer. "I'm committed. Just wait." She didn't really understand what the rush was; if Bockscar had waited a hundred years for their eyes to meet across the depth of the well behind Victory Community Church, what difference would another day make? A month, even? She kept promises just as well as secrets, after all.

Every day you wait is a day you waste, said Bockscar, because even without being co-mingled, Bockscar knew all the shadowy ditches of her brain where she hid her doubt. *As a human you only have so many days to spend.*

"What are you doing?"

Ashlyn snapped her hand back from the flame. The sun was up, a full inch of the candle had melted, and Steph was standing in the doorway with her toiletry bag, looking confused. Maybe a little scared.

"I'm meditating. Trying to manifest the things I want. It's actually really calming, you wanna try?"

Steph took two hesitant steps toward the tub, but jolted back when the flame flicked toward her. Ashlyn wanted to ask if she saw something in the fire she didn't like—or maybe just couldn't think of anything to manifest—but Steph was busy peeking out the little window above the tub at the driveway below.

"Looks like you guys have a visitor," Steph whispered.

"Pastor Delbert," Ashlyn said, without needing to look. Bockscar had shown her what was happening outside: Ranae rushing to greet the pastor, because Bart—her father, her daddy—could no longer find it in his body to rush anywhere, anymore. "He's very worried about us. He thinks we're infested."

"Infested? With what, termites?"

Oh dear. Steph really *hadn't* been raised under the eye of God. "Since when do termites throw plates?" Ashlyn tried to keep it in but the mischievous giggle sprang from her throat like a snared fish yanked from a lake. "What kind of termites do they have in that city of yours, Steph?"

She had not meant to let Steph see her true, laughing face, the one with the eyes and mouth held open wide enough to drink the world. But she must have, because Steph's skin color shifted from the pink of slightly-undercooked shrimp to the gray of unoxidized beef. She didn't answer the question—just brushed her teeth so quickly and quietly that Ashlyn could practically see the wall of cold come down between them.

She knows, Bockscar said. *She's going to tell*.

"It doesn't matter," Ashlyn whispered. It didn't matter because she had seen the quiet dismay with which the family had listened to Steph's stories the day before—the insane man on the bus with the blood-crusted machete, her roommate the witch who was dating a vampire, the job that didn't require her to cover up her tattoos, her insistence that crime in the city wasn't that much of a problem. Anything she said now would be tainted with the stench of sin.

You're smarter than you look, Bockscar said, *which is why you're perfect*.

"What'd you say?" It was Steph. Ashlyn had forgotten that she was still hovering over the sink, her lips frothy with toothpaste suds. She definitely looked worried now, clenching onto the sink with her free hand like she was afraid the floor might suddenly collapse beneath her.

"I said it doesn't matter what Pastor Delbert thinks," Ashlyn replied, and touched her finger to the fire. As Bockscar promised, there was no pain. "He's just a pilot without a map. A witch without a broom."

Steph went quite still. It was funny—when she first met Steph at Aunt Bonnie's funeral, the very first thing Ashlyn noticed about her cousin was her spiritual dullness. Dead as a doorknob, Bockscar would have said. And yet even she could sense her beloved's presence. This was the miracle of Bockscar's power.

Later that morning, Ashlyn walked in on the tail end of Steph's attempt to tell the grown-ups downstairs about her "strange behavior." Her poor cousin had no concept of the language she'd need to make them understand the urgency of her warning—she rambled about candles and Pastor Delbert and the bus she'd rode in on, a mess that not even Pastor Delbert was able to link to his nightmare—and all it took for Ashlyn to flip the board was a specific cut to the jugular: "Steph asked me not to tell. She's been seducing married men."

In the cloud of profanities and flailing limbs that followed, Steph actually looked feral. Or maybe just betrayed.

—————◄O►—————

Possession occurred in four stages, Pastor Delbert explained, and Cousin Steph was in the third: obsession. "The demon probably found her in the city," he said over coffee in the breakfast nook, "and had her oppressed by the time she got to Palfrey. And now it's driving her, like a favorite car. The fact that it's moving so quickly means it's very strong. Do you see that? How extremely *wicked* it must be?"

The man is in denial, Bockscar whispered in Ashlyn's ear. It took all her self-control to bite down on the smile threatening to creep out of her mouth. Fortunately, no one seemed to notice the tremble except for Cousin Wyatt, who'd been looking at her askance all afternoon.

"We should send the girls away," Ranae whispered to her husband. "Amity, at least."

Ashlyn glanced over her shoulder at the sprite sitting in front of the refrigerator, looking very small in her half-grown bones. She wondered if some deep part of that child knew; sometimes Amity got so quiet around her, tucking her limbs in like she was afraid Ashlyn might grab one. Maybe she'd overheard an odd conversation. Maybe she didn't know quite what to make of it. Maybe she'd decided she'd better not mention it if she wanted to play it safe.

Pastor Delbert clucked his tongue in exasperation.

"That poor girl," he said, pointing up the stairs at the guest bedroom where Steph was tied to the bed, "needs all the spiritual reinforcement she can get right now. Isn't family the closest thing we have to God's love? She needs all of you."

It was a rhetorical question, but Aunt Bex still grunted in approval, clearly invigorated by the opportunity to be a soldier for God. She was pacing with her sleeves rolled up, eager to get back into the guest bedroom and bear down on Steph's body while Pastor Delbert and Bart chanted Bible verses.

Bart nodded, clenching his fist. "Absolutely. Everyone stays."

Wyatt scooted his chair back. He ignored his mother's scolding for the first time in his life, fought the deeply-nested instinct to obey Pastor Delbert, kept his eyes strictly away from Ashlyn as he got up. His fear was so profound that he would not stop for anyone—no one except Amity, that is. When his gaze snagged on the little girl sitting in front of the refrigerator he paused, and Ashlyn would not have stopped him if he'd grabbed Amity's hand and taken her someplace cool and safe. But he didn't. The same doubt that had always made Wyatt such a disappointment to his mother got the better of him, and he just ran.

Clever boy, Bockscar said.

Later that night, when the screaming started up again, they shut Amity in her room and told her to pray for Cousin Steph.

"Love her as God loves you," Pastor Delbert said before closing the door.

Never mind that Amity didn't love Steph at all; didn't love anyone except her father and sister. But then again, who *did* love Steph, that crumpled sack of waste and decay? Her father and Ranae were just scared of falling into that fetid marsh. Aunt Bex just wanted to beat the Devil out of somebody.

Like Amity, Ashlyn wasn't allowed near the exorcism. She busied herself with preparing overnight oats for their Sunday breakfast until Aunt Bex yelled down the stairs to "bring salt up" and Ranae was too catatonic to respond. Ashlyn, ever the good girl, grabbed the jar of rock salt and made her way to the guest bedroom, trying not to look too giddy.

Upstairs, her father stood in the hallway with his forehead pressed against the wall while Aunt Bex and Pastor Delbert huddled inside the guest bedroom. They moved away from the bed when Ashlyn entered, grabbing the salt jar and telling her to take the dirty sheets to the washer.

"Don't get too close!" they hissed, like Steph was a chained alligator.

Yes, a chained alligator—like the kind they had on display at Gator Gauntlet over in Haightville. Pastor Delbert said their job was to stop the demon from taking full possession of Steph by making its human home as uncomfortable as possible. Bockscar claimed to be going mad from the fluctuating energy in the house, the clashing waves of terror and bloodthirst, but Bockscar was a catastrophist of the Old Testament kind. Ashlyn could tell that Pastor Delbert's prayers and violence were only having a negligible impact on the target. The collateral damage, though, was vast.

"I know it's you," Steph whispered while Ashlyn crouched next to the bed, gathering up the bloody sheet.

Steph would have been stupid if she *didn't* know by now, Ashlyn thought, taking in the delicious scent of rust.

"You want to know how I knew?" Steph coughed, her back jerking into an arch that certainly looked painful, if not paranormal. "The story you had me tell your family. About the crazy guy on the bus. You knew about it before I ever said anything. There was no way. No way you could have known."

Ashlyn cocked her head to the side. "I'm the only one that loves you, now that your mother's dead."

Upon hearing this, Steph's bruised face further twisted into a wretched sob.

It bothered Ashlyn. Looking back on this moment later, though, she would not remember exactly why.

Say yes, Bockscar whispered—but this time, Ashlyn finally realized that all of Bockscar's pushy nudges weren't commands. They weren't even invitations. They were pleas.

———◦———

While she was checking Pastor Delbert for a pulse, pressing her delicate spider-fingers against his vomit-encrusted neck, Ashlyn wondered why Bockscar had chosen her. Out of everyone in this tight-knit community, she couldn't have been the first to find the old well, vine-draped and moss-covered. To feel the call to answer the question it posed, like a partially-blocked sign. To look in.

Now that they were united, Ashlyn knew why she'd been the one. She could see the dozens of eyes—brown eyes, green eyes, blue eyes, cataract eyes—that had peered into the well's darkness and blinked at the shadow that was her new other half. But none of them held the imagination or ambition necessary to craft the better life that was the core of the American dream. In fact, Bockscar had waited so long for someone like Ashlyn to emerge from the simple-minded pack that he almost lost hope and left town entirely.

But then came that hot summer afternoon with Ruth Gaddie, when Ashlyn caught sight of the well and became so fixated on its darkness that Ruth never asked her for help again. There was no need to imagine what Bockscar saw when her face leaned over the bricks and looked through the spiderwebs; Ashlyn could now see for herself.

The passion, her nerve endings whispered, sparking with Bockscar's touch.

Pastor Delbert was dead. The last to go, a lucky victim of his diligent commitment to Steph's exorcism. If he'd gone home at a reasonable time, he wouldn't have been invited to sleep on the couch instead of driving back in the dark. If he hadn't woken up with the Jacobsens this morning, he wouldn't have eaten any antifreeze-oats.

Now reassured, the passion carried Ashlyn's feet through the Jacobsen family house, the house she'd once considered her home, the house where people she once professed to love had died at her hands.

Their hands? No, her hands.

Those hands that were now collecting the snacks and wallets she would need for her time on the road. Her fiery eyes swept over the corpses in the breakfast nook without mercy or sentiment. Their souls were in the void now. The big empty. There was nothing left to feel.

From the staircase came the sound of dragging against carpet.

Steph. Looking like hell itself had spat her out. The beatings had left her unable to stand, so she was army-crawling like a recruit, or a baby. She must have chewed her way out of the binds, then thrown herself off the bed so she could wriggle toward the stairs. Had she also seen Bart's body in the hallway, choked on its own vomit on its way to the bathroom? Had she heard little Amity wail?

Yes, Ashlyn and Bockscar knew. *Yes, she had*.

And when Steph felt the heat of Ashlyn's eyes, she bellowed. "Please!" she cried. "Take me!"

No surprise registered on Ashlyn's face. The human spirit is compelled to freedom, both Bockscar and Ashlyn knew.

An urge that belonged to Bockscar sprang up inside Ashlyn's body to take the broken girl on the upper landing, at least for a little while. Stuff her in the backseat of the pickup. Wait for her wounds to heal. See if she could be useful, maybe; see if she could blossom within the fire like her cousin, maybe.

But those thoughts drowned in the crush of Ashlyn's sweet, treacherous sea.

For I am a jealous God, the cells that had once been Ashlyn explained. But that was on the inside. On the outside, the rosy face that had once belonged to Ashlyn turned toward Steph's broken form, and the slender hand that had once belonged to Ashlyn waved goodbye.

When Mercy is Shown, Mercy is Given

Angela Sylvaine

Behind every smile, there's teeth.
Confucius

M ercy's new teeth emerged the day of the funeral. Her mother, Faith, always said a smile was the best accessory. Not only does that bold flash of pearly white increase a girl's loveliness, but it serves as a barrier against any offense. No matter what unkind phrases are flung, what unwanted touches delivered, that wide swath of gleaming teeth stops a girl's tongue from lashing out with words that would turn her ugly and unladylike.

Faith lay nestled in the white satin of a mahogany casket. Though wearing her favorite tweed Chanel suit and freshwater pearls, she looked distinctly underdressed without her trademark smile. As much as Mercy tugged and pried at Faith's lips, they wouldn't budge from the stiff line that scarred her face thanks to mortician's glue.

Mercy decided she'd smile enough for both of them and stretched her lips wider and wider as she greeted the mourners who milled around the reception area of the funeral home. Her grandma pulled her aside—not to bemoan the loss of her daughter and Mercy's mother, not to comfort and connect through shared grief, but to scold her.

Grandma Grace lifted the netted veil obscuring her face and gripped Mercy's arm tight with fingers like claws. "You look like a clown with that grin. See your aunts, your cousins? Those are proper ladies."

Her aunts, Patience and Charity, had two grown daughters each, and all were present. Every one of them wore designer dresses and small smiles infused with just a hint of sadness. They gathered in clusters throughout the room, listening attentively as their husbands told stories, delivering food or refills of drinks, ensuring the children were seen and not heard. They reacted to jokes from the men, but never made a sound, their laughter no more than a carefully controlled motion of the face.

Mercy was the youngest of them all, barely nineteen, and being in the presence of those perfect women made her feel like an ugly duckling among swans. So, she watched and mimicked their appropriate smiles, making sure to get that sad tilt of the eyes and to show only the barest glimpse of teeth.

She kept that smile plastered to her face until her jaw ached and her cheeks twitched under the strain—when the pins that held her hair back in a tight chignon stabbed into her scalp. When she caught her mother's friends whispering about the wrinkles that creased Faith's mouth, her forehead, the corners of her eyes. When Aunt Charity insisted she'd move in with Mercy the following day, because she couldn't possibly be trusted to care for herself.

Her control almost snapped when Uncle Ray, Charity's husband, slid his hand down the curve of her ass and pinched Mercy through the crepe silk of her black dress. Her fingers curled into fists, and she barely managed to keep herself from punching him in the face. The only thing that stopped her was the thought of how repugnant her mother would find such behavior.

Instead, Mercy smiled at her disgusting pervert of an uncle, and pain sliced through the roof of her mouth. She was used to hiding discomfort, so her pleasant expression held steady, but the first salty tear of the day leaked from her eye and rolled down her cheek, slithering over her top lip.

Probing the throb behind her front teeth with her tongue, Mercy found a new, bony growth. Not blunt and rounded but pointy, with a barely-serrated edge, better suited for a shark than a lady. A spike of fear stalled her breath at the possibility her mother had manifested from beyond the grave to punish her, to keep her in line.

But the rusty flavor of her own blood conjured only memories of lucky pennies, treasured and tasted and rubbed flat. The pain gave way to comfort, this strange new secret thing in her mouth somehow easing the pressure in her chest. By the end of that long day, Mercy had what felt like a dozen new teeth lined up in a row behind the ones she displayed to the world.

Sitting at her mother's vanity that night, stomach full of blood and sympathy casserole, she tilted her head back and opened her mouth wide to examine the shards that had erupted from the roof of her mouth. A normal person would call an ambulance, seek medical treatment, but she'd been raised to always hide her imperfections. Besides, the new teeth felt *right*.

Her mother's framed photo of a beaming Marilyn Monroe watched from atop the vanity. Faith loved to quote Marilyn's words–that there was so much to smile about. She'd slapped Mercy the day she asked why, then, Marilyn had swallowed a handful of pills. Mercy grabbed the photo and dropped it in the trash can, feeling freer than she had in years.

She crawled into bed that night and prayed. Not for her mother to miraculously return, but for her new set of sharp teeth to stay, that they were real and not some sort of hallucination.

Mercy knew when she woke that her prayers had been answered, copper from the bite of her new teeth into the flesh of her tongue. They had folded back, tucked themselves up against the roof of her mouth, but when she nudged them with her finger they flexed forward, as if eager to chew and bite.

On a normal morning, her mother would tell her what to wear, monitor what she ate, ensure she'd planned a productive day. But Faith was gone, so Mercy climbed into a luxuriantly hot bath her mother wouldn't have approved of and let the sadness and relief and guilt wash over her, never once crushing them down or forcing a smile. She didn't bother with her hair or makeup, got dressed in her comfiest flannel pajamas, and ate until her stomach was actually full.

When the doorbell rang in the early afternoon, Mercy checked her reflection in the entry mirror out of habit and winced at the sight of herself, unkempt and feral. Faith would never have tolerated such an appearance, but she reminded herself her mother was dead.

Straightening her shoulders, Mercy opened the door.

Mrs. Phillips from next door stood in the hall wearing a prim knee-length dress and holding a cloth grocery bag.

"You poor thing, did you sleep at all?"

She stepped inside, though Mercy didn't invite her.

Mercy closed the door with a sigh and followed the woman through the open floor plan apartment, past the contemporary living room devoid of photographs or knick-knacks and into the combination dining room-kitchen.

"I slept very well, actually." Except for the dreams, well, perhaps nightmares of her mother standing over the bed, prying at her mouth.

"Pshh, of course you didn't." Mrs. Phillips pulled chicken breasts, fresh vegetables, and a variety of fruit from the bag and placed them in the fridge next to Faith's single servings of plain yogurt. "I'm sure you don't even know what to do without her, do you?"

"No, I don't," Mercy said, and that was true. Her mother had always controlled every aspect of her life, every moment of her day, leaving Mercy feeling a bit lost. But she found the thought of finally deciding for herself–becoming her own woman–exhilarating.

"Come on, let's get you cleaned up." Mrs. Phillips took Mercy's elbow and led her toward the hallway that held the bathroom and the apartment's three spacious bedrooms.

She yanked her arm free. "I've already bathed and dressed."

"Well, you look a mess. I know Faith wouldn't have tolerated you walking around like this, and accepting company in such a state, no less."

Her new teeth flexed forward in her mouth, obvious to her but still hidden from view. "My mother is dead, and I think you should leave."

Mrs. Phillips clutched the collar of Mercy's dress. "You're behaving extremely poorly, young lady, and grief is no excuse."

It was Mercy's turn to grip Mrs. Phillips elbow and steer her back the way she'd come. "Please go."

She crossed her arms. "Not before you apologize."

Mercy knew it would be easy to apologize, had been doing so for minor misbehaviors and perceived sleights every day of her life as far back as she could remember.

"You apologize," she said instead.

Mrs. Phillips gaped. "For what?"

"For barging in here uninvited, insulting me, and assuming you have any right to tell me what to do."

Mercy barely registered the movement of Mrs. Phillips' hand before it delivered a stinging slap to her cheek.

"You little brat!"

Mercy lunged, and Mrs. Phillips' eyes went wide as she stumbled backward into the wall beside the front door. She turned her face, narrowly avoiding Mercy's snapping jaws, which caught the woman's understated gold hoop, tearing it free from her ear.

Mrs. Phillips screamed and clutched the side of their head, blood trickling through her fingers and down her wrist.

"You bit me!"

Mercy plucked the earring from her mouth and shoved it into Mrs. Phillips' free hand. "You assaulted me after refusing to leave my home, and I accidentally caught your earring while trying to get you to leave. Isn't that right, ma'am?"

Mrs. Phillips swallowed, watching Mercy with wide eyes, and finally nodded.

Mercy opened the door, and Mrs. Phillips rushed to her own apartment, slamming the door. "Thank you for the groceries," Mercy called, smirking.

"What was that all about?" a familiar voice asked, and she turned to see Grandma Grace and Aunt Charity standing in the open elevator at the end of the hall.

———◆◇◆———

Mercy licked at her lips, tonguing away the remaining hint of Mrs. Phillips' blood. "Grandma, Auntie, how nice of you to stop by." She pasted on her old, polite smile, though it pained her.

Grandma Grace and Aunt Charity, clad in mourning black with hair expertly styled, strode past her and pushed into the apartment. Charity pulled a rolling suitcase behind her, and Mercy remembered the comment from the funeral about them moving in. Panic churned her stomach.

She followed them inside, closing the door, and bared her teeth briefly in the mirror to ensure her new set wasn't visible, but of course they weren't.

"You really shouldn't have troubled yourselves, I'm doing fine," she said.

Charity strode down the hall, toward the guest room, and Mercy ran after her.

"I'm doing fine on my own, you don't—"

Grandma Grace guided her toward the kitchen, urging her to sit down in one of the dining room chairs.

"Relax, dear, I'll make you some tea."

Mercy gripped her hands in her lap and took a deep breath. They were just worried about her, just being supportive after the loss of her mother. She couldn't fault them for that.

"That would be nice, thank you."

She watched the door of the guest room, waiting for Aunt Charity to emerge, telling herself that one night of company, even two, would be fine. Mercy would just have to prove to them that she really could take care of herself.

Cups and saucers clattered behind her as Grandma Grace pulled them from the china cabinet. Mercy knew there would be no milk or sugar, though she preferred both, because Grandma was a purist and insisted tea should not be corrupted by unnecessary calories.

The electric kettle whistled as Charity emerged from the guest room, a duffel bag slung over one shoulder, as if she were on her way to the gym. She took a seat beside Mercy, dropping the bag to the floor. Charity's face was pinched, wrinkles carved around her eyes and mouth, and Mercy reminded herself that her aunt had lost a sister. She reached out to squeeze the woman's hand.

Charity squeezed back. "It's going to be okay, sweetheart."

Grandma Grace set a cup in front of each of them, then took her spot at the head of the table, the spot that had once belonged to Faith.. Mercy sipped her bitter tea, holding back the grimace that wanted to emerge.

Her grandma and aunt drank in silence, casting looks at Mercy.

"That woman, your neighbor, looked quite upset. Was anything the matter?" Charity asked.

Mercy gulped down the rest of her tea, then set the cup back in the saucer, her hand trembling. Her new teeth flexed, and she reminded herself no one else could see them, no one else knew, not even Mrs. Phillips. "She was just upset about mother. They were close."

"I thought I saw blood. Did she injure herself somehow?" Grandma asked.

"No," Mercy said, her voice too loud. She cleared her throat. "I mean, I don't think so, not that I saw."

Charity heaved a sigh. "You can trust us, you know. We're family."

"I know." A flush crept up her chest, her face. "Is it hot in here?"

A wave of dizziness blurred her vision. "I don't ... feel so good." She put her elbows on the table and cradled her head in her hands, though it was very bad manners.

Charity leaned over and unzipped the duffle bag, rifled around.

Straining to focus, Mercy watched as Charity pulled a small case from inside and opened it to reveal a scalpel, pliers, and a vial of clear liquid.

"We're going to help you, sweetheart, don't you worry."

Mercy gripped the edge of the table and stood, but only managed a few steps before her legs wilted, and she crashed to the tile floor. "What ... did you give me?"

Grandma Grace crouched beside her. "It's better this way, dear. Just go to sleep."

"No." Mercy tried to sit up, but her body wouldn't obey. Tears pooled in her eyes as they drooped, and she lost consciousness.

———◆———

Mercy came to slowly, her mind clawing its way out of the fog. A throb filled her mouth, and she probed where her new teeth should have been with her tongue, but found only a row of small, empty holes.

"No," she whispered, trying to move her head, but a strap across her forehead kept her immobile.

She opened her eyes, blinking away the blurriness. The light in the room had changed, transitioned from day to night, and a familiar chandelier, the one over her dining table, hung directly above her. Her wrists and ankles were held in place by more leather straps. She yanked at the restraints and screamed, "Let me go!"

"Hush, now, you're going to be just fine." Charity bent over her, a reassuring smile on her face. She wore a blood-splattered plastic poncho over her clothes. "I know it hurts, but it'll be worth it when we're done."

"My teeth," Mercy croaked, a tear leaking from the corner of her eye.

"Our curse." Grandma Grace appeared on the side of the table opposite Charity, clad in an identical poncho. Her previously perfect curls were a tangled mess, and a dark splatter marred her face. She peeled off her rubber gloves and held up a small white, triangular object stained red at the wide end. One of Mercy's new teeth. "They've plagued the women of our family for hundreds of years, as far back as anyone can remember."

"You ... knew?" Mercy asked, her mouth dry, lips cracked and caked with dried blood.

"We suspected at the funeral." Her aunt's nostrils flared. "Smelled the blood on your breath. And when we saw that woman, that neighbor, we knew you'd snapped."

"You had no right to take them from me." Mercy's throat tightened, thick with ten times the grief she'd felt at the loss of her mother. "I could've learned, I *would* have learned to control myself."

"No, dear. They control you, make you into a monster," Grandma said.

"In a few days, once they're gone for good, you'll become the woman you were meant to be. One of us." Charity smoothed one hand over Mercy's sweat-soaked hair.

"A few days?" she asked, eyes widening at the prospect of being strapped to the table for that long. They'd already taken her precious teeth, what more torture did they have planned?

Charity frowned. "Those demon teeth don't go easily, they grow back, usually just once or twice, but sometimes more."

Mercy sobbed with relief. They weren't gone. They'd come back like those of great white sharks, falling out or lodging themselves in prey, then growing brand new again.

"It'll take at least a few hours for the next set to come in," Grandma Grace said, slumping into one of the dining room chairs.

Mercy sucked in a breath, realized what they were saying. That they'd keep taking her teeth until none grew back. "Please, don't do this. I need them. I promise, I'll be good, I'll control myself." She yanked at the restraints holding her head, her wrists, but they wouldn't budge.

"I felt that way, too, at first. Took four rounds to pull mine, and I wept like a baby every time. We all did," Charity said. "But once they're gone, you won't have to fight to keep control. Look at me, at your cousins, don't you want to be content like we are?"

Mercy thought of those perfect women at the funeral, hovering at the edges of conversations, waiting to be of use. Never really smiling or laughing. Never getting angry but never happy, either. "No. I want you to let me go. Right. Now."

Grandma pressed the tooth she'd been holding into Mercy's palm. "This is the only tooth you keep, just this one. It is for the best, dear."

Mercy curled her fingers around the tooth in her hand, squeezing tight, letting the serrated edge dig into her flesh and draw blood. She couldn't fathom going back to who she'd been trying to be, couldn't imagine ever being content as one of them.

"Come on, Mom, you need some rest," Charity said, taking Grandma's arm to help her stand before turning to Mercy. "We'll be back to check on you in a few hours, and this will all be over soon enough."

The two left Mercy tied to the table; their fading footsteps followed by the gentle click of a closing door. Pain sliced through Mercy's palm, but she didn't drop the tooth, *her* tooth, only clutched it tighter. Blood flowed, coating her skin down to the wrist, and she tugged again at the restraint, felt her hand slip through up to the joint of her thumb. The roof of her mouth tingled before filling with fresh agony as new teeth emerged, one by one.

She gripped the souvenir tooth between her finger and thumb, angling her wrist until she felt its sharp tip bite into the strap. Hand wrenched and aching, she sawed at the leather. Sweat rolled from her forehead to sting her eyes, but she didn't stop, nibbling at the restraint one millimeter at a time.

The leather snapped and she gave a relieved gasp, before clamping her mouth closed and lying still. There was no sound, no sign of her grandma or aunt returning. She reached up and unbuckled the strap on her forehead, then freed her other wrist and her ankles.

Pain plagued her mouth, her hand, every spot that she'd rubbed raw struggling against the restraints, but she smiled. Mercy was free. She hopped from the table, peeking down the hall at the closed guest room door. Her new set of teeth tingled with anticipation. Those women, her family, meant to crush her true nature, to mold her into a harmless guppy, docile and inoffensive. But Mercy knew her purpose now, what she was meant to be. A shark.

Thirteen Ways of Not Looking at a Blackbird

Gordon B. White

I.

I am a baby boy. In the bathtub, looking out, past my mother as she cries and holds the already wet washcloth to her eyes. Over her mouth. I am looking into the full-length mirror on the bathroom door.

I see no one.

I do not see my father.

A severed hand floats in the air. Drops of blood fall to the floor, splattering out on both sides of the border between the linoleum and carpet.

No one says, "I've sinned again," as my mother cries.

II.

Our house is the one that looks perfect from the sidewalk. The siding is new, the eaves and trim are painted and bright. Gutters clean; lawn thick and green; picket fence as straight and white as teeth. The dogwoods bloom like big, pink brains in the spring, and lavender and bee balm fill the yard with their scent in summer.

Inside, we have a door in the kitchen that doesn't lead anywhere. It has three silver locks—three like the bears in the story. A papa, a mama, and a baby, just like us.

At night, after she's finished reading me fairytales and has turned off my light, I lie in bed and listen to the family of locks in the door to nowhere tumbling open and then back into place. The house shakes as heavy footsteps don't go downstairs. Sometimes, too, I can almost hear other sounds that drift up through the ducts as if the house is singing sadly.

I ask Mama about it. I get her to hold her breath and put her ear to the vents.

She tells me that I can't hear anything. That there's nothing there. After that, I don't hear it anymore.

III.

Because Daddy works until all hours, Mama is the one who tells me how the world works. Even though she didn't get to go to school, her parents' house was filled with towers of books and old papers that seem to grow from the piles of trash on the floor. She tells me that everything she knows, she knows from reading. I don't realize it until later, but she's closer to my age than Daddy's.

I can ask her almost anything. How the flowers grow, how the TV works, why is the sky blue?

"Did you know," she tells me, "that hundreds of years ago, back in olden times, people didn't have a word for 'blue'?"

I shake my head.

"And without a word for it, they couldn't see it. Not like we can. I mean, it was there, right? But it wasn't something they could make sense of."

I can ask her almost anything, but only almost.

The sting of her hand is like a hornet and the red shape of it burns through my cheek. "You don't ask about what he does," she says. "You don't see nothing, you don't say nothing. Never. Never ever. You understand?"

Too stunned to cry, I nod.

"Good," she says. "Good boys keep their mouths shut about business that ain't theirs. They don't talk about it and they don't think about it." She shakes her head. "Bad boys go to hell."

IV.

I am in the kitchen and it is dark. The clock radio says 12:47 in red numbers that glare like eyes from the counter. I waited until the light beneath Mama's door was off before sneaking down the hallway, each step seeming to find a new groaning board beneath the carpet, but I am now barefoot on the linoleum. I search the cabinets, trying not to make alarms of the pans and glass baking dishes as I search for the marshmallow cereal I know Mama has hidden. I'm only allowed one bowl on Saturdays, but I want to feel the chalky sugar on my tongue.

From behind the door to nowhere, I hear a crash. A thin gleam seeps from under the base of the heavy door, and there is a pounding that grows and grows behind it, as if rising from the empty ground beneath. The silver locks in the door tremble and shake, falling out of place.

The door to nowhere opens.

A naked woman with hair in a matted fury stands there. Blood drips from her fingers and mouth, black in the clock radio's red glow, but she stands illuminated from behind by the light from a place that doesn't exist. She sees me and her eyes widen; her mouth splits as if to laugh.

"Door?" she asks.

I point off down the front hall. She runs, bare feet smacking against linoleum, then wood.

But now there is a howling. A storm rising from nowhere. As it bursts into the kitchen, I don't recognize the center at first, with its face marred by four ragged furrows. My eyes sink into those finger-deep trenches and I fall back as the maelstrom rages—screaming, shouting, smashing.

By now my mother is here, too, and when she says his name, I realize the storm is my father. The angry face coalesces back into the one I know, as it does, the thunderhead and ferocious gale which shook the kitchen dissolve into a fog.

I run back down the hall to my darkened bedroom. I am wrapped in a blanket and staring out the window for that naked woman, wondering if she's cold, when the red and blue sirens descend.

V.

The law doesn't know what to make of Mama. A dozen people think real hard about what she didn't do and didn't not do with no one, then throw up their hands. The man in the black robe says she can go but God help her. He shakes his head, says God help us all.

I can go too, because I'm so young, but part of it is that I have to talk with a lady once a week for what seems like forever.

Mama tells me it's not a lie to say you don't remember if you really don't, so if I forget I won't be a bad boy or liar. Good boys don't talk about their fathers and mothers to strangers. Good boys don't say what they did or didn't see.

Good boys don't say yes or no. They just say that they don't know, sorry.

VI.

We change our names from nothing to something. I was so small that even the internet doesn't know who I was when I wasn't. And we have to leave the house, of course, but we make a go of it. Mama works, I go to school, and we come right back afterwards to wherever we happen to be that week.

Sometimes, though, when I look in the mirror or in the empty TV screen or the window at night, I see a face I don't recognize. Or more precisely, I don't. I ask Mama about it, but she says nevermind. It's nothing.

It isn't that we never talk about it. In fact, Mama talks everything over with me again and again until I remember clearly the empty wheelbarrows being pushed out of the basement I didn't know we had. Until I remember garbage bags with nothing in them, carried out from the freezers by men in masks and white paper suits.

My memory of the old house is a field of yellow caution tape around empty holes between bushes of lavender and bee balm that nobody dug, men and women kneeling beside them and covering their faces with their hands in front of nothing at all.

VII.

My daddy is still alive. I ask about him sometimes, where he is, but the sting of Mama's hand is a reminder I don't often need. She'll never take me to see him, she says, because while she'll always love him, we need to move on.

We stay with her parents for a while—Gammy and Pawpaw—but they look at us like strangers. I hear them lock their bedroom door at night and Gammy would rather sit on the porch until Pawpaw gets home in the evening than be inside when just Mama and I are there.

"But you must have known?" Gammy says one night at dinner.

"I didn't see anything," Mama says.

"You must have guessed," Pawpaw says. "I mean, so many—"

"I didn't see nothing!" Mama slaps her hand against the table, rattling the silver. She stands but doesn't leave. "I told them all, there was nothing to see."

Pawpaw looks at me, squints. "What about you?"

I look at Mama and she glares at me hard enough across the table that my cheek begins to blister in the shape of her palm.

"No," I say. "Nothing."

"Not even that night? The one that got away?"

I don't even need to look at Mama. I just shake my head and look at the chicken on my plate. Pawpaw spits on the floor by his boots.

"Disgusting," he says.

VIII.

I look in the mirror and try to make sense of what I see, but I don't have a word for who or what that is. The context is missing. The parts are all there—eyes, nose, lips, ears. They hover in an arrangement that should be recognizable, but the parts just don't connect. I feel like a Mr. Potato Head without the potato.

In one of Pawpaw's towers of paper I find an old library book on muscles and bones. The cover is like nothing I've seen before, a woman's face and neck and shoulder leaning over as if asleep, while the secret world of roads and rivers beneath the skin is opened up. It makes me feel heat and shame, but it comes to live beneath my bed. At night, I push against and peel back myself where I can, trying to figure out what I am made of, inside and out.

Back in the mirror, I grow obsessed with the connective bits and parts in-between, learning new terms for the parts of the strange face I see: glabella; infraorbital furrow; infraorbital triangle; nasolabial furrow; philtrum; chin boss. In the fairytales Mama used to read me, having the true names always seemed to be a kind of magic and, for a few moments as I point and name them in the mirror, I think that I can almost see how I fit together.

But no. The longer I look, the more I realize the pieces are there, but something inside is missing.

I say my name over and over as I stare my reflection in the eye, as if catching the goblin in darkness and calling out "Rumplestiltskin!" might bind him. But that's not my name—it's not either of them.

I try to picture what it is inside of me, but I have nothing. So many memories of nothing and the things that no one did.

IX.

I dream I am back in our old house. I am in the kitchen, sitting at the table in front of a bowl of marshmallow cereal but I can't find my hands to lift the spoon. As I'm sitting there, though, nothing begins to move around.

The front door slams, but when I peer out, the hall is empty. The heavy clomp of approaching boots shakes the walls and I want to cover my ears with the hands I can't find, but as the footsteps stamp around me in circles, I can see nothing.

Frozen, I watch the refrigerator door open. A red and white can floats from inside, hisses as the tab is pulled, then pours out into thin air only to vanish. The cabinets swing open and closed; the faucet off and on; the knife drawer in and out. Then the crash of footsteps stops right beside me.

Over the years with the lady from the court, I have become accustomed to the sensation of being held down and pinned open as if for examination, and that familiar weight comes to rest on me in the dream, even though no one is looking at me. The needles of it burn like Mama's slaps, but deeper and redder, piercing outward from somewhere within. Then nothing ruffles my hair like a faithful dog and shuffles over toward the door to nowhere. The three locks obediently twist themselves over one by one. The door swings open on its own.

A sudden crash of thunder and the kitchen is dark, as if the power went out. The only light comes from the doorway to nowhere. Another crash, but this time *she* is there.

All I can see now is that woman who came up from nowhere. She is standing there, naked and angry, bleeding as if born back from the nothing below, and my heart begins to race. There is something in me that is responding in a way I don't have words to describe—a wash of heat and shame and desire and anger all at once.

I wake up and the sheets are a mess.

The look of repulsion on Mama's face when she does the laundry in the morning says everything.

I still have the book on anatomy I stole from Pawpaw and I laboriously study all the terms to try and understand the woman. All the folds of muscle; the deposits of fat and flaps of skin; a tree of bone decorated like Christmas in tinsel of nerves and veins. Naming the parts helps me feel steadier, more in control. At least while I'm awake.

But I have the messy dreams again. Again. In a fit of shame, I cut the sheets into little pieces and throw them away, only to get caught a few days later stealing a replacement set from K-Mart. They call Mama to come take me home, but she won't even speak to me.

X.

I want to tell someone, but I can't. I open my mouth real wide sometimes when I'm in bed or when I'm at my new school or even when I'm in the bathroom. I just open it and try to make a sound that would maybe trick the words into coming out, but it just curdles into the most sickening groan.

The lady I'm made to talk to asks me what I remember. I tell her nothing. She asks me what I dream about. I tell her nothing. What do I want to tell her? About the nothing, nothing, nothing, but she only smiles and checks something off on a piece of paper.

We meet less and less as the years go by, until by the time eighth grade is done, the lady says I'm doing just fine. She says we don't need to talk about it anymore.

XI.

I can feel my body changing. My brain too, squashed and pulled as the plates of my cranium shift. I am still having those dreams, and when I go to school or the store or the park, I can't help but see that woman. Hiding behind trees. Down the bread aisle. Again and again—naked, bleeding, about to laugh.

I find out Daddy is dead more than a month after it happened when I hear some kids at school talking about it. At first it doesn't register because the name they use wasn't his real name. Butcher. Strangler. Ripper.

The words they use don't reconcile with what I didn't see.

But as they keep talking, one of them says his name—the one I used to share with him before Mama and I changed it—and for a moment I'm a baby boy again. I am in the house where we don't speak of things Daddy doesn't do.

But there's a hole there in the house. A swirl of shadows that moves in and out of doors, through the halls, around me in the kitchen. A blank spot the size and approximate shape of my father, but one that bends light around until it slips by unnoticed. Did Mama and I talk so much *around* it that I became blind?

Well, the other kids are talking *about* it now. Saying the police had to dig up the backyard. They start listing out the pieces that were found and the ones that weren't. They're describing the tools. The basement behind the door with the three silver locks.

I can almost see through that haze in my memory of the house. I can almost ...

The others say that one night, one of the girls fought back. She got away. Unlocked the door.

And like a flash of lightning, there she is standing among them. Proud and naked and my father's blood on her hand and in her mouth. That same surge of desires and distress washes over me, making me hot and dizzy, but now I see clearly. I see that she's the one who took it all away from us. She's the one who talked. Who is talking now. Who—

When the teachers finally pull me off the other students, they drag me to the principal's office, but first we stop at the boys' restroom and they tell me to wash my face.

I splash it and feel a sting, but looking into the mirror I see nothing. There is nothing on my face or behind my eyes. I hear whispers from no one behind.

The principal is yelling at me, demanding to know just who I think I am. What are my parents going to say?

I can only laugh.

Nothing. I'm no one's son.

XII.

"Mama," I say, "I need to talk to you."

There's a hole I have to fill. A gap in my understanding.

"I need to talk about Daddy."

"No," she says.

"Please? I don't know if what's wrong with me is like what—"

A crash like thunder.

"Nothing was wrong with him. Nothing is wrong with you, too."

XIII.

I may as well be a baby boy. In the shower, looking out through steamy glass, past the hooks where white towels hang like the damp skins of childhood ghosts. The side of my face burns, hot and red in the shape of a hand across my cheek. I am looking into the full length mirror on the bathroom door.

I see no one.

I do not see myself.

A severed hand floats in the air. Drops of blood fall to the tile floor, splattering out across my toes and mixing with the water as it swirls down the drain.

No one says, "I've sinned again," as no one cries.

Welcome to the New You

Gwendolyn Kiste

It's just before noon on a Sunday when Evelyn's doppelganger replaces her at brunch.

She's sipping a Bloody Mary at the table one minute, telling me about her upcoming vacation to Myrtle Beach. Next to us, Chrissy and Violet listen in, the four of us together like always, gathered around our favorite table on the restaurant patio.

Then Evelyn's phone rings, and she excuses herself from the table, dashing down a nearby alley where she can take the call in peace. As we wait for her to return, our glasses of ice water sweating in the heat, another smiling Evelyn passes our table and disappears the same way.

"Wasn't Evelyn already down there?" I ask, and everyone around me goes quiet, the truth settling into our marrow.

Without a word, we know what this means.

On instinct, I jolt from my seat, ready to warn her, but Chrissy's hand is suddenly on mine, pinning me in place.

"You simply have to stay with us, Laura." That familiar fake smile plastered on her face. "You haven't told us about your vacation plans this summer."

I wrench away, my gaze set on the alley, but another hand is on me. Violet's this time, gripping my wrist.

"You need to try the smoked salmon," she says, and she's grinning too.

When I glance around, others at the surrounding tables are grinning the same way, and they're standing now. Together, they block my way, because I should know better. You aren't allowed to speak of what's happening to Evelyn, and you certainly aren't allowed to stop it.

The whole world wobbles around me, my breath twisted in my chest. There's a tiny yelp from the alley, so small, so pitiful that nobody else probably hears it but me.

When it's over, the thing with Evelyn's face emerges and takes the chair next to mine.

"Sorry I'm late," she says with a giggle.

We're sitting with a stranger. This isn't our friend, not anymore. Everyone in the restaurant knows it. They also won't say a word about it.

So we drink a pitcher of mimosas and dine on veggie frittatas and discuss the weather—clear, blue skies, for what it's worth—and when it's over, we go on our way like this is any other afternoon.

"Goodbye, Evelyn darling," Chrissy says, always more than eager to play along with the charade.

After they've left, I double back and slip into the alley, searching every crevice. Except there's nothing left. No body. Not even a drop of blood. The most I can find is a shallow puddle covered in white bubbles, as pale as seafoam.

My hands shaking, I reach down and run my fingers through it. The substance dissolves at my touch.

"I'm so sorry," I say, but nobody's around to care.

I'm still shaking when I get home to my husband.

"I don't want to go out to brunch with them anymore."

He laughs and kisses my forehead. "You always say that."

"I mean it this time," I whisper, and I want to tell him all about it. About the doppelganger and the alley and the way I never asked for those people to be my friends, that it just seemed to happen. Everything in my life just seems to happen, the years disappearing in the rearview mirror, every choice feeling like happenstance.

Every day, waiting to meet my own doppelganger.

But I don't say any of that. I just smile back at him and close my eyes and do my best not to scream.

———◦———

It might come for you in your sleep. Or when you're sitting behind your desk, daydreaming at work. It might stroll right in through the front door of your house and take your seat at the supper table.

But there's one rule that everybody remembers, an iota of comfort to the damned: Your doppelganger only gets one chance to replace you. Once you meet, it will be over soon, no more than a day or two before one of you wins out.

"It's you or them," the kids at school used to whisper when they were sure no teacher was around. "You can't both exist in the world at the same time for long."

What happens when you finally meet is anyone's guess. Nobody ever tells you how to kill your doppelganger, because that would be unseemly. In a way, it's like killing yourself.

There are other rules, too. Like how no one is allowed to help you. This is your battle alone. It would be rude for anyone to take your glory.

Once upon a time, they used to teach about it in schools. An old instructional video on a grainy VHS, one that your health teacher made all the kids watch in the fourth grade, everyone snickering like it was some kind of joke instead of a possible death sentence. But at least in those days, they told kids about it.

Then some purse-lipped senators got other ideas.

"It promotes deviance," they said, as though this was our own fault, like we were all asking for it.

As though you could simply pray your doppelganger away.

"Besides," they added, "there's no need to upset the children with such talk."

But since nobody discusses it, that means not everyone even knows it's coming. So when the quarterback on our high school football team saw his double for the first time, he just stood there, slack-jawed, staring back at himself. He didn't even have time to scream before it was over.

And it turns out the doubles aren't exactly like you, not in every way. Our school, the shoo-in favorite, lost the state championships thanks to the doppelganger's middling throwing arm.

"Maybe they should have shown us that video in fourth grade after all," I said, but my mother only hushed me.

But now nobody mentions it. Not parents or schools or even your pediatrician. Growing up, my friends would only murmur about it on the playground or at sleepovers, all of us gathered around in the dark, like we were telling ghost stories about our own dubious futures.

"They say it doesn't even hurt," the other girls would whisper. "The doppelganger makes sure you never feel a thing."

That sounded like bullshit to me, but what did I know? Most kids at school met their doppelgangers early, half of them surviving it, the other half replaced, not that you could always tell the difference. Yet here I am, the tail end of my thirties slipping away, and still no sign of my own face anywhere I look.

———◆———

It's six months before I see another doppelganger. It belongs to Violet this time, and we meet it when we're walking to an art opening on the North Shore.

"Everyone's going to be there," she's telling me when a shadow engulfs us. It's got a hand on Violet before we even see its face. In a flash, they tumble to the sidewalk, and there's a crack of bone and blood everywhere.

"Laura, please," Violet wheezes, grasping for me, and I want to help her, even though I shouldn't.

Even though she wouldn't let me help Evelyn.

I back away, and the world wobbles again, the same way it did that day at the restaurant, as though the air itself is ready to unravel. I remember what the children used to say when I was young.

You can't both exist in the world at the same time for long.

And these two don't exist together for long. Violet, the real Violet, pries off the thing with her face, her hands wrapped around her own throat. I kneel next to her, my hands stacked atop hers, both of us tightening our grip until we hear it—one sharp snap of the neck, and her doppelganger goes limp in our embrace.

We huddle together, staring at it. The dead Violet who isn't really Violet at all.

Then at once, there's nothing left to look at, bones going soft as pudding in our hands. She yelps as we drop what's left of it, flesh melting into a clear liquid, the liquid dripping down to the concrete. When it's over, Violet's facsimile is no more than a puddle covered with ashen foam.

Violet heaves up a gag. "Is that what would have happened to me? Would I have dissolved like that?"

"I don't know," I whisper, but it's a lie. That's exactly what would have happened. That's what happened to Evelyn.

Because we can't think of anything else to do, we keep walking to the art opening. Inside, there's an avant-garde light installation and laughter and cheese and crackers on a wooden charcuterie board. It's a friendly evening filled with friendly faces, and I've never felt more alone.

Evelyn is here too, the replacement Evelyn. Everyone but me has gotten used to her by now. She waves from across the room, but I pretend not to see her.

Chrissy, on the other hand, is unavoidable. "Hello, darlings," she says, cornering us by the punchbowl and kissing our cheeks. She hesitates, inspecting Violet. "What's different about you? A new perfume?"

"Nope," Violet chirps, her eyes wide. "Nothing new at all."

But Chrissy doesn't believe her. All evening, she keeps her eyes on us, tracking our every movement. I invent a flimsy excuse to head home early.

Later that night, with my husband murmuring softly in his sleep next to me, I grip my phone and scroll through message boards online. It's hard to find any threads dedicated to doppelgangers—sites always scrub them away—but sometimes, you can catch a glimpse of a conversation that's slipped between the cracks, evading moderators, existing quietly in the white noise of the internet.

I've seen it. Today outside of work. I saw my double.

time to fight! good luck man

But what if I don't want to fight? What if I run? I could catch the next flight out of town. What happens then?

sorry you don't get a choice

But why not?

because it doesn't work like that, you gotta fight or else everything will fall apart

"Everything will fall apart," I say, remembering how the world wobbled earlier tonight. Like the universe might come undone around us.

In the morning, I'm still thinking about the message board and about Violet's double when my cell phone rings. It's Chrissy.

I exhale a heavy sigh before answering. "Hey, what's up?"

"You weren't supposed to do that, Laura." Her voice is strange and impassive on the other end. "You know you aren't allowed to help her."

The whole house goes still, and for a moment, I swear it feels like she's watching me.

"I have no idea what you're talking about," I say, smiling through a sneer.

"Then don't let it happen again," she says, her words sharp as a switchblade at my back. "There are rules about that sort of thing."

I hang up without saying goodbye. For the rest of the day, I keep telling myself it doesn't bother me, but she's right. There *are* laws against it, though nobody really has to enforce them anymore. These days, the threat is enough to make us all comply.

It was enough to make me comply when I came home from college to find that my mother was someone else.

"What's wrong, Laura?" she asked when I walked in, bookbag slung over my shoulder. She smiled, all her pale teeth gleaming back at me.

It was the slightest of differences, no more than a whisper behind her eyes. The doppelgangers are good, I'll give them that. They almost have you doubting yourself.

"You're not her," I said, edging away, my stomach whirling. "You're not really my mother."

"You're being dramatic, darling," she said, and that smile never faded, not even when I screamed, my throat going raw, or when the screaming finally gave way to sobs or when the sobs fizzled into defeated silence.

I haven't been home to visit her in years, but she still calls once a week and pretends she's my mother. "I don't understand why you don't want to see me," she says, and all my flesh prickles at the sound of her vacant voice.

It's after midnight when I hear my husband stirring in bed next to me, and I suddenly can't help myself. I blurt out the question I've wanted to ask for years.

"Did you meet yours?"

"Laura," he says, and even in the dark, I can tell he's rolling his eyes. "You know you aren't supposed to talk about things like that."

"But I want to talk about it."

A long moment, the shadows pressing nearer.

"Yes," he says at last. "I met mine."

My chest constricts. "When? Before we were married?"

"Right after."

I can't breathe. "Why didn't you tell me?" I ask, and my hand searches for his beneath the blanket.

"It didn't seem important." He turns away from me. "Besides, it happens to everyone. You know that."

"It hasn't happened to me," I whisper. "Not yet."

"Sweetheart, please go to sleep."

And with that, he closes his eyes and dozes off. I sit up next to him, staring into the shadows, wondering which version of my husband I'm lying next to. The one I married or the one I've become accustomed to.

After everything, I wonder if I'd even notice the difference.

I'm nearly forty years old when I finally meet her.

It's another Sunday brunch, all of us guzzling booze on the patio, my life nothing more than an endless rerun. I don't want to be here, but these days, it doesn't seem like there's anywhere else to go. My friends won't listen. Neither will my husband. The best I can do is smile and wait for it.

And suddenly, I don't have to wait any longer. It's such an odd thing, to see your own face staring back at you from across a crowded street. She's loitering in front of the barbershop, wearing the same outfit I am. Black blazer, black boots.

I blink once, and she's gone, vanished into the throng.

"What's wrong, Laura?" Violet giggles and tosses her long hair out of her eyes. "You look like you've seen a ghost."

"No," I say, because it's much worse than that.

You can drive out a ghost. You can't drive out yourself.

At home, my husband and I sit on the couch, the figures on the television flashing across our faces. He doesn't ask why I'm quiet. He's busy talking about work, the rigamarole of spreadsheets and internal audits and accounts payable. During a commercial break, there's a strained silence between us before I finally say it.

"She's here," I whisper.

"Who?" he asks, not looking at me.

"My double."

His eyes are on me now. "Come on," he says. "You know we can't discuss this."

"Why not?" I glance around, my voice splitting apart. "Who's here to stop us?"

"Laura." He says my name as if it's a weapon. "I didn't bother you when it happened to me."

I sink back on the couch, defeated. "But I wish you would have. I wish you would have told me everything."

"It'll be fine," he says and pats my leg. "I promise you. They're not as strong as they look."

"Then why do they win sometimes?"

He doesn't answer me. We go to bed an hour later without speaking again.

"Will you miss me?" I ask in the dark, but he's already fast asleep.

———◇———

I wait for her in the morning, long after my husband has gone to work. He kisses me on the forehead before he leaves.

"Everything will be fine," he promises, and I nod as though I believe him.

My doppelganger, however, isn't like the others. She doesn't sneak up on me when I'm distracted on the phone or pounce on me from the shadows.

Instead, she rings the doorbell.

My heart clenched tight, I answer, even though I see her through the peephole, even though I know what's to come.

After all these years, I just want to get this over with.

Except that's not what happens.

We simply stand on either side of the threshold, staring at each other. The air shimmers around us, but neither of us seems to notice. We're too preoccupied with inspecting our own face, these uncanny mirror images.

At last, I exhale a sigh. "Would you like a cup of tea?"

We sit together at the table, sipping Earl Grey. She adds honey to her cup. I like honey too, so I do the same.

"I don't think we're supposed to do this," she says, and takes another gulp of tea.

"I won't tell anyone if you don't." My nervous hands tapping on the table. These hands that match hers. "Where do you come from?"

She only shrugs. "It's sort of like being born. You don't remember it."

"What do you remember?" A quiver in my voice. "Do you have all my memories?"

She nods. "I think so."

This chills me, the way I'm already alive and waiting inside her. Like the world doesn't even need me anymore.

"What happens if I don't kill you?" I drift toward her, close enough that I could reach out and snap her neck. Or she could snap mine. "And what happens if you don't kill me either?"

She shakes her head. "I only know that's against the rules."

"Whose rules?"

"I'm not sure."

The walls vibrate softly around us, and I wait for it. The moment everything starts to unravel.

Except that doesn't happen. Not yet anyhow.

I look hard at her, at the way her brow furrows, just like mine does. "Would you like to stay for a while?"

I set her up in the attic where my husband won't find her.

Once she's nestled in the corner, I start to head downstairs, but I can't help myself. I glance back once at her. "I've been waiting a long time to meet you."

"I've been waiting for you, too," she says, and these aren't the words we're supposed to speak. We should be built to loathe each other. To tear out the other's throat. To do everything we can, so that we can be the only one. The only Laura.

But with the air still glinting like a spray of diamonds, we keep looking across the attic, watching the other's face.

And we smile.

———◇———

A sinkhole opens up the next morning on the outskirts of town. I hear about it on the radio after my husband's already left for work.

As if on cue, Chrissy appears at my front door. She knows everything, even if nobody ever tells her.

"You haven't been answering your phone," she says. "Is there something wrong?"

I force a smile. "Nothing at all."

She asks to come in for coffee, but I tell her I'm all out.

"Come back later," I say, and that seems to pacify her for now.

My double peers through the curtains, as Chrissy strolls to her car. "She's one of us. A replacement."

"I know," I say.

———◆———

The following day, after the local DJ announces a tornado has destroyed the next town over, Chrissy returns, and she brings backup, Evelyn and Violet flanking her.

"Aren't you going to invite us in?" they ask, their voices practically in unison.

My body broadens, blocking the doorway. "Not today," I say.

"Brunch on Sunday then." Chrissy smiles at me. "Don't be late, Laura."

That night, before my husband gets home, my double and I settle on the sofa, watching the evening news. There's been an earthquake on the other side of the state, and the worst wind storm in a century, too.

"This is our fault," I say, even though it shouldn't be. We're hurting everyone by not hurting each other.

She draws nearer to me, and my own face is suddenly resting on my shoulder. "What are we going to do?" she asks.

"If you don't know," I say with a laugh, "then neither do I."

———◆———

By the fifth day, half of downtown has burned to the ground in inexplicable fires, and another sinkhole has cracked open up at the county line.

The air trembles, as we stand together at the attic window, flames flickering in the distance.

"Should we just get this over with?" she asks. "For their sake?"

"No," I say, my jaw set. "They wouldn't help us. They won't help anyone."

A long, ragged sigh. "We won't last much longer like this," she says, and I know she's right.

I reach out in the darkness and entwine my fingers with hers. She squeezes my hand tight.

Neither one of us is willing to let go.

On Sunday, I do exactly what I promised. I show up at brunch. Both of me.

With a grin, I drag an extra chair to our usual table, and my doppelganger and I sit side by side. There isn't a sound in the entire restaurant, the patio gone still as the grave.

This is against the rules, and we all know it.

"Laura," Chrissy murmurs, but she doesn't say anything else. Everyone is pretending they don't see us, these splitting images right in front of their eyes.

The world is wobbling again, everything unraveling at once. First, the nearby traffic lights go dim. Then the sky follows suit, all the color leached out of it.

Violet leans in, her mouth a harsh line. "You know what you have to do," she says, and she's talking to my double, not to me. I'm not sure if she can't tell the difference, or if she just doesn't care.

Either way, both of us ignore her, sipping our mimosas until the pitcher's gone dry.

"Can we have a spot of tea?" I ask, and someone brings us a kettle before the whole restaurant clears out.

Evelyn flees first, followed by Chrissy and Violet, and everyone is eager to go with them, cowering on the other side of the street, still watching us. Somebody must have called my husband, because he soon joins them, his face pallid and lined.

"Laura, stop this," he pleads, his gaze darting between me and my double. He can't tell us apart after all.

We know what's expected of us. The snap of a neck. The jab of a knife. Anything quick. Anything that would end this. That would be the polite thing to do. The right thing to do, according to them.

Only it's not what we're going to do. Instead, we stay at the table and finish Violet's plate of sunny-side-up eggs. The sky dips lower, and a gray acid rain materializes, scattering the spectators, their screams echoing long after they're gone.

Everything will fall apart. That's what the world promised us unless we did what we were told. What nobody seemed to understand is that everything fell apart long ago, way before we were here and could be blamed for it.

The edges of the restaurant are crumbling now, bricks sloughing off in jagged chunks, and I'm glad to see it go. Maybe what's to come isn't paradise. Maybe it'll be a new beginning or just a plain old ending. But at least it's not this place.

And at least it's our choice.

As something rumbles through the earth, strange and primordial, my doppelganger looks at me, her eyes shining bright. The same way my eyes are no doubt shining.

"Would you like a cup of tea?" she asks.

"Of course," I say, and together, we smile, as what's left of the world dissolves around us.

Content Warnings

Cire Perdue: sexual assault, body dysmorphia

These Small Violences: poverty shaming/classism, child on child physical violence, adult on child physical violence, blood, poisoning

The Dust Collectors: body horror, invasion/defilement of a safe space

The World of Iniquity Among Our Members Is the Tongue: death of a parent, starvation, verbal abuse, graphic injury, cannibalism

An Inherited Taste: domestic violence, emotional/psychological abuse

Anger Management: physical violence, emotional abuse

The Man Outside: stalking, violence

As the Silence Burns: misogyny, assault, sexual assault (off page)

Acid Skin: misogyny, threat of sexual assault, mild gore

The Guest Room: threat to child, kidnapping

Echthroxenia: none

See Something Say Something: violence (including against children), death of a parent

When Mercy is Shown, Mercy is Given: death of a parent

Thirteen Ways of Not Looking at a Blackbird: child abuse (physical and emotional), death of a parent

Welcome to the New You: body horror violence

Author Bios

Ariel Marken Jack lives in Nova Scotia. Their fiction has appeared in *Beneath Ceaseless Skies, Dark Matter Magazine, Prairie Fire, PseudoPod, Strange Horizons*, and more. They curate #sfstoryoftheday, review short-form speculative fiction for *Fusion Fragment*, and muse about food and death in SF for *Psychopomp.com*. Find their work at arielmarkenjack.com.

J.A.W. McCarthy is the Bram Stoker Award and Shirley Jackson Award nominated author of *Sometimes We're Cruel and Other Stories* (Cemetery Gates Media, 2021) and *Sleep Alone* (Off Limits Press, 2023). Her short fiction has appeared in numerous publications, including *Vastarien, PseudoPod, LampLight, Apparition Lit, Tales to Terrify,* and *The Best Horror of the Year Vol 13* (ed. Ellen Datlow). She is Thai American and lives with her husband and assistant cats in the Pacific Northwest. You can call her Jen on Twitter @JAWMcCarthy, and find out more at www.jawmccarthy.com.

Shenoa Carroll-Bradd writes horror and fantasy from her home base in sunny southern California. Her short fiction has appeared in dozens of anthologies and been featured on several podcasts. When not writing, she enjoys strength training, learning German, and smothering her senior dog with affection. Find her at facebook.com/sbcbfiction and sbcbfiction.net.

D. Matthew Urban hails from Texas and lives in Queens, New York, where he reads weird books, watches weird movies, and writes weird fiction. His stories have appeared in *Bitter Apples, Ooze: Little Bursts of Body Horror,* and *Shredded: A Sports and Fitness Body Horror Anthology*, among other venues. He can be found on Twitter @breathinghead or on the web at https://dmatthewurban.com.

Nadine Aurora Tabing is a writer, designer, artist, and shiba inu enthusiast who lives in the Pacific Northwest. Her work has been published by *Strange Horizons, Reckoning, Utopia Science Fiction,* and Clarion West as part of their 2022 Flash Fiction Contest. She can be found online at nadinetabing.com, on Twitter as @suchnadine, and on Mastodon via @suchnadine@wandering.shop.

J. Rohr is a Chicago native with a taste for history and wandering the city at odd hours. To deal with the more corrosive aspects of everyday life he makes music in the band Beerfinger. Currently, he writes articles for the websites Horror Obsessive and Film Obsessive. His Twitter babble can be found @JackBlankHSH.

Simone le Roux is a third culture kid still figuring out the culture part. A lover of all things dark and creepy, but not the cold, she has settled in Cape Town where the temperature never dips lower than chilly, but the rainfall is spectacular. An admirer of all mildly wasteful things, she has a neuroscience degree that she only uses to fact-check her own stories and an accent from a country she barely remembers. You can follow her adventures on Twitter @SimoneLives.

Sara Tantlinger is the author of the Bram Stoker Award-winning *The Devil's Dreamland: Poetry Inspired by H.H. Holmes,* and the Stoker-nominated works *To Be Devoured* and *Cradleland of Parasites.* She has also edited *Not All Monsters* and *Chromophobia.* She is an active HWA member and also participates in the HWA Pittsburgh Chapter. She embraces all things macabre and can be found lurking in graveyards or on Twitter @SaraTantlinger, at saratantlinger.com and on Instagram @inkychaotics.

Marisca Pichette's work has appeared in *Strange Horizons, Vastarien, The Magazine of Fantasy & Science Fiction, Fantasy Magazine, Flash Fiction Online, PseudoPod*, and *PodCastle*, among others. Her speculative poetry collection, *Rivers in Your Skin, Sirens in Your Hair*, is out now from Android Press. She spends her time in the woods and fields of Western Massachusetts, sacred land that has been inhabited by the Pocumtuck and Abenaki peoples for millennia. Find her on Twitter as @MariscaPichette and Instagram as @marisca_write.

R.L. Meza is the author of *Our Love Will Devour Us*, published by Dark Matter INK. She writes horror and dark science fiction, and her short stories have appeared in *Nightmare, Dark Matter Magazine*, and *The Dread Machine*. Meza lives in a century-old Victorian house on the coast of northern California, with her husband and the collection of strange animals they call family.

Avra Margariti is a queer author, Greek sea monster, and Rhysling-nominated poet with a fondness for the dark and the darling. Avra's work haunts publications such as *Vastarien, Asimov's, Liminality, Arsenika, The Future Fire, Space and Time, Eye to the Telescope*, and *Glittership*. "The Saint of Witches", Avra's debut collection of horror poetry, is available from Weasel Press. You can find Avra on twitter (@avramargariti).

Nadia Bulkin is the author of the short story collection *She Said Destroy* (Word Horde, 2017). She has been nominated for the Shirley Jackson Award five times. She grew up in Jakarta, Indonesia with her Javanese father and American mother, before relocating to Lincoln, Nebraska. She has two political science degrees and lives in Washington, D.C.

Angela Sylvaine is a self-proclaimed cheerful goth who writes horror fiction and poetry. Her debut novel, *Frost Bite*, is forthcoming from Dark Matter INK, and her debut novella, *Chopping Spree*, an homage to 1980s slashers and mall culture, is available now. Angela's short fiction has appeared in various publications and podcasts, including *Apex Magazine, Dark Recesses,* and *The NoSleep Podcast.* Her poetry has appeared in publications including *Under Her Skin* and *Monstroddities.* You can find her online at angelasylvaine.com.

Gordon B. White is a Shirley Jackson Award- and Bram Stoker Award-nominated writer of horror and weird fiction. He is the author of the collection *As Summer's Mask Slips and Other Disruptions* (2020), and the novellas *Rookfield* (2021) and *And In Her Smile, the World* (with Rebecca J. Allred, 2022). Gordon's stories, interviews, and book reviews have appeared in dozens of venues. You can find him online at www.gordonbwhite.com or on Twitter @GordonB-White.

Gwendolyn Kiste is the three-time Bram Stoker Award-winning author of *The Rust Maidens, Reluctant Immortals, Boneset & Feathers,* and *Pretty Marys All in a Row,* among others. Her short fiction and nonfiction have appeared in outlets including *Lit Hub, Nightmare, Best American Science Fiction and Fantasy, Vastarien, Tor Nightfire, Titan Books,* and *The Dark.* She's a Lambda Literary Award finalist, and her fiction has also received the This Is Horror award for Novel of the Year as well as nominations for the Premios Kelvin and Ignotus Awards. Originally from Ohio, she now resides on an abandoned horse farm outside of Pittsburgh with her husband, their excitable calico cat, and not nearly enough ghosts. Find her online at gwendolynkiste.com.

Acknowledgments

We would like to thank our incredible authors: Ariel Marken Jack, J.A.W. McCarthy, Shenoa Carroll-Bradd, D. Matthew Urban, Nadine Aurora Tabing, J. Rohr, Simone le Roux, Sara Tantlinger, Marisca Pichette, R.L. Meza, Avra Margariti, Nadia Bulkin, Angela Sylvaine, Gordon B. White, and Gwendolyn Kiste.

We would also like to thank Olivia Steen for the wonderful *No Trouble at All* cover design

Thanks so much to R.J. Joseph for the incredibly thoughtful foreword.

Thanks to Alex Ebenstein and Brandon Applegate for both moral support and practical publishing advice.

And lastly, thanks so much to all of our Kickstarter backers: Kyle Tolan, E.A. Barnaby, Pernicketypony@gmail.com, Paul Foster, Charles W. Younts III, E. Catherine Tobler, Adam "Chili" Stevens, Kamo, Megan Kiekel Anderson, Devin Jessup, Carter, Chelsea Pumpkins, Brandon Applegate, Tiffany Michelle Brown, Elizabeth R. McClellan (@popelizbet), K.C. Mead-Brewer, Justin Montgomery, Christina Wilder, Dana Vickerson, Susannah PK, Lynne Walter, Damon Barret Roe, Sonora Taylor, matthew wend, Kenny Endlich, Adrian, Laura Lusardi, Mom and Dad, Dan Bjork, Ryan Marie Ketterer, Teresa B. Ardrey, Kathryn Reilly, Jonathan Wlodarski, Dave Urban, Jolene Jones, Patrick Malka, Alex February, Ben Long, Bridget D. Brave, Alba Arnau Prado, Wayne R., Sarah Duck-Mayr, Angie Steiner – strangersights.com, Jim Brownrigg, jaredlkuntz

@gmail.com, Paige Holland, Alex Ebenstein, Laura Kemmerer, Phil Keeling, Ryan E. Johnson, Patrick Barb, Mr. Kitty, Derek Anderson, Donyae Coles, Susan Jessen, Kevin Lemke, mindyleereads, Kenneth Skaldebø, Ashleigh H., Bec Snow, William Jones, Alan Lastufka, Katrina Carruth, Whitney Trang, Jude Deluca, Christi Nogle, Aurora Biggs, Sofia Ajram, Aryn Huck, Ava Dickerson, Nicole Conge, Jess Leigh Unrein, Iesha Elias, Max Booth, Justin Lewis, Seana Bice, Kelsey Christine McConnell, Mady Hays, Anthony R. Cardno, Sam Cowan, Tom Coombe, Ryan Power, Arnela Bektas, Grayson Sheldon, Zach & Zeb Hauptman, Cary Morrison, Cassandra Daucus, Marissa van Uden, Austin Hofeman, Luke W. Henderson, Dustbound, Illeana A., Cynthia Gómez, Lisa Westenbarger, Laura Blackwell, K Petrin, Nolias Kane, Stina Marie Patton, Becca Futrell, Emmy Teague, Michael Cieslak, Cat A., Sarah Fannon, Frederick Rossero, Cathy Green, Lesley Conner, Anna Bender, Isaac Sherry, Alex X., Rachel L. Peterson, Rain Corbyn, Zack Fissel, Corey Farrenkopf, Finneus Earnhardt-McClain, Ariel Reser, Sarah, Natalia Tylim, Liz Eddy, Rebecca Cuthbert, Allison Funneman, C. Ess, Kelsea Yu, J.B. Robinson, R.L. Summerling, Jonathan Mendonca, Shelley Lavigne, Chris McCartney, Basile Lebret, Ben Trigg, Threnody Cassidy, Samantha Kolesnik, Jared N, Alice Austin, Elizabeth Williams, summervillain, J.V. Gachs, Lauren Carter, Andy @midwesterngent3, Nathan T, Steve Pattee, DJ Cameron, J.C. Levimil, Justin Moritz, Giusy Rippa, Edward De Vere, Theresa Derwin, Boris Veytsman, Joanne B Burrows, Kyle Nolla, Alan Mark Tong, Scott J. Moses, Lor Gislason, J. Jason Lau, Mab, Windi R. LaBounta, Kelly Hoolihan, Steven Patchett, Victoria Nations, Daniel & Summer Dawn Smith, Meredith Morgenstern, Taliesin Neith, Stephen Howard, Melissa Cox, Olov Livendahl, Mia T, Laurel Hightower, Jimbo Slice, dave ring, Tiffany Morris, Edward Kane, Jessica Enfante, Sebastian Ernst, Anatolia Russell, Rachel Bolton, Lou, Dan Hill, Amara Moore, Mallory A. Haws, Sergey Kochergan, Ria Hill, and Lord Byron.

Other Books from Cursed Morsels Press

Bitter Apples

Cursed Morsels Press presents tales of teacher horror from Corey Farrenkopf, Emma E. Murray, Cynthia Gómez, Christi Nogle, D. Matthew Urban, Eric Raglin, and Aurelius Raines II. These writers have worked in the profession, and while their stories are fictional, the darkness they explore is all too real.

In *Bitter Apples*, you'll find students' ghosts haunting classrooms, desperate teachers joining cults, zombies plaguing underfunded schools, and more. The institution of education is rotting. How will we survive its horrors?

Shredded: A Sports and Fitness Body Horror Anthology

Reader beware! This sports and fitness body horror anthology is dangerous. Side effects include monstrous steroid transformation, concussion-induced madness, possession by jock ghost, death by yoga cult, and more. Read with caution!

Featuring seventeen reps of terror by Nikki R. Leigh, Tim Meyer, Brandon Applegate, Red Lagoe, Caias Ward, RW DeFaoite, Mae Murray, D. Matthew Urban, Charles Austin Muir, Joe Koch, Michael Tichy, Rien Gray, Robbie Burkhart, Eric Raglin, Matthew Pritt, Madeleine Sardina, Alexis DuBon, and J.A.W. McCarthy.

Antifa Splatterpunk

Fascism didn't die in 1945. Its grave was only temporary. Rising again, this undead ideology shambles into the present, gathering power and spreading destruction wherever it goes.

This monster stalks the pages of *Antifa Splatterpunk*, in which sixteen horror writers explore fascism's many terrors: police wielding strange bioweapons against the public, white supremacists annihilating their enemies through dark magic, and TV personalities vilifying all who defy the rising fascist tide.

But these stories are resistance: Nazi-killing demons, Confederate-slaying witches, and everyday people punching fascists in the teeth. Among the gore is a glimmer of hope that one day this monster will return to its grave and never rise again.